SWAT TEAM AND MISS ROBIN HOOD

The Men of Five-0 #2

Dixie Lynn Dwyer

LOVEXTREME FOREVER

Siren Publishing, Inc.
www.SirenPublishing.com

A SIREN PUBLISHING BOOK
IMPRINT: LoveXtreme Forever

SWAT TEAM TWO AND MISS ROBIN HOOD
Copyright © 2011 by Dixie Lynn Dwyer

ISBN-10: 1-61034-695-5
ISBN-13: 978-1-61034-695-5

First Printing: June 2011

Cover design by *Les Byerley*
All art and logo copyright © 2011 by Siren Publishing, Inc.

Printed in the U.S.A.

PUBLISHER
Siren Publishing, Inc.
www.SirenPublishing.com

DEDICATION

To my readers, your continued support keeps my fingers on the keyboard and my creative mind flowing with more and more ideas each day. I hope to create heroes you will dream about long after the book has ended and heroines you can empathize with and ultimately adore.

SWAT TEAM TWO
AND MISS ROBIN HOOD

The Men of Five-0 #2

DIXIE LYNN DWYER
Copyright © 2011

Prologue

The beat of the drum, the sound of the music, and the rumbling of the bass appeared to be Lilly's sole focus. Lilly loved to dance. She loved music, but she didn't like showing off her body. Melissa knew that as she watched her co worker strut her stuff. Melissa tended bar and that was good enough for her. She watched Lilly, mesmerized by her moves and desire to earn some extra cash. In her mind she imagined what Lilly was saying to herself to keep up the act. Lilly wiggled her hips. The crowd of men roared as the tassels on her nipples danced in sync to the music. Years of starving, not knowing where the next meal was coming from, gave her tight abs. Lilly told Melissa that herself. Her stomach had shrunk, and she had gotten used to that nagging ache and that rumbling inside her belly. Melissa knew that feeling all too well herself. Running on the streets, dodging cops and crooks, gave her muscular and toned arms as well as the definition needed to look athletic. The only parts of her body that weren't so small were her breasts. Melissa was grateful for them, but also knew that her breasts made her a target for horny men.

The beat of the music increased, and so did Lilly's dance moves. She gripped the pole, humped and ground against the steel bar, pretending it was a man's body and she was riding his cock. The crowd roared as hard, masculine fingers shoved bills in the waist of her purple sequin thong. She had to twist away to the right before that one slimeball Jerry got a good hold of her.

"She sure can dance that one," Chuck blurted out as he downed his shot of whiskey and looked at Melissa as she tended bar.

"Yeah, she sure can," she replied then looked back at Lilly. Jerry was trying to get his hands on Lilly. Melissa hoped that Spike was close-by. She looked around the bar for the burly bouncer and caught sight of him. He was on top of it as usual.

Jerry flirted with just about everyone. He had been after her, wanting to show her that a pole was nothing compared to a real man. She dodged his slimy hands when she worked behind the bar, and Lilly would dodge his slimy hands now that she was dancing just about naked in front of a crowd of a hundred or so.

Lilly looked up towards the crowd and smiled. That brought on another wave of excitement. Melissa followed Lilly's line of sight as Lilly wiggled her hips away and spotted Tom. Tom was loaded and most importantly was a fantastic tipper. He didn't mess with leaving dollar bills. He dropped hundreds like they were dollars. The words to the music were sexy and filled with connotations about a woman blowing men's minds. She had the body, she had the desire, and she had the motivation. Lilly was desperate to get out of the stripping business and settle down with a real man. It just hadn't happened yet. Lilly squatted down low, practically pressing her pussy to the dance floor, which caused one group of young men, closer to Melissa's twenty-two years of age than Lilly's thirty, to roar with excitement and tumble over chairs to press money to her thong. They had fives and tens, but Tom had a fistful of hundreds as he pointed his finger for her to move closer so he could tip her well. Lilly placed the palms of her hands in front of her and did a slow body slide forward as she held Tom's gaze with her deep brown, seductive eyes. She had told

Melissa that she practiced the look for hours in the mirror. She was told that the look would make a priest come in his pants.

Her 34Cs pressed against the floor then up, practically in Tom's face, but she didn't release her look. She raised her ass up high, which caught a few smacks from the hands of brazen men until good old Spike, the bouncer, set them in their place. The song was ending soon, Melissa could tell. She looked at Tom as he tipped Lilly. He was an attractive man, a little overweight, and came to clubs like this to release stress and pressure from work. As a bartender, she learned her clientele well. Especially the wealthy ones.

He said something to Lilly. Melissa was too far away to tell what he had said but Lilly looked happy. Then Tom touched her left breast with one hand as he placed a fistful of bills in the front of her thong against the small patch of material that covered her pussy. The song was ending as Lilly leaned forward, touched his chin with her finger, then rose from the floor in a smooth, seductive manner. She hurried to the back of the stage to exit as cheers and screams filled the club.

Melissa felt her own heart race as the crowd's excitement filled the air.

"You should be up there, sweetheart." Chuck interrupted her thoughts. Melissa felt her cheeks warm as she shied away, placing a strand of hair behind her ear.

"I don't think so."

Chuck laughed. "Better for me that you don't," he added, taking a sip of the beer she just got him.

"Why is that?" she found herself asking, feeling a bit insulted that he would say such a thing. For a moment she ignored the other two men that approached the bar, looking to be served.

He locked gazes with her.

"With your body, my entire paycheck would go to you every week."

She was thankful for the compliment, and then she smiled.

"Thanks," she replied then walked away to serve the other patrons.

Chapter 1

Melissa struggled to keep the two bags from falling as she climbed the stairs to the third-floor apartment. Her body ached from a full week of double shift at the bar. If her mamma could only see her now, she'd be beside herself knowing that she worked at a strip club and tended bar to a bunch of sexually overzealous men. She'd also have Melissa sent to a nunnery. God rest her mamma's soul, and God help her survive these last three deliveries.

As she approached the final doorway to the third floor, she used her knee to balance one bag as she strategically opened the door with the free hand. Then she amazingly got through the metal door without dropping a single bag. As she turned the corner of the hallway where Celine and her two young children resided, she noticed the man in the dark suit exit the doorway to Celine's apartment.

He eyed her from head to toe, and yeah, she was used to it, but that didn't mean she liked it. He practically undressed her with his eyes, and if the bags weren't about to fall, she would have commented on his rudeness. Men could be such pigs. Sex, sex, sex was all that ever seemed to be on their minds. Instead of remarking verbally, she gave him the once-over as if he was nothing to look at. The jerk got the hint and hurried down the stairwell.

Melissa set the two bags down on the floor and knocked on the door.

"I told you that the answer is no!" Celine exclaimed as she pulled the door open, obviously expecting the man who had just left to be there again.

"Oh, geez, I'm so sorry, Mel. I swear I thought it was that asshole from the bank again. Come in, come in, please," she insisted then grabbed one of the bags off the floor.

Melissa knew that by now, the three babies, Zack and Kelly, four-year-old twins, and Zoey, her five-year-old, were sound asleep.

"Is everything okay?" Melissa asked as she looked at Celine reclasp the two top buttons on her blouse.

"Yeah, fine. I guess since I'm behind in payments still on the old house mortgage, they send a collector in person. Wasted trip on his part, though. I don't have an extra dime."

Melissa sighed. She knew all too well what it was like to have very little financially. Struggling from check to check had been the way she grew up. She knew what it felt like to not know where the next meal was coming from or if there would even be another one.

She placed her hand on Celine's shoulder. "What can I do to help?"

"Oh, please, Mel, you've done so much so far. You got me that job, the babysitter, and a place to live so the kids and I wouldn't be scared in the shelter anymore. I wouldn't dream of asking for more."

"You're not asking, I'm offering"

"You have your sister's kids to handle. You do enough for everyone around here. How about doing something for yourself?" Celine asked as she began to help Melissa unpack the groceries.

"Oh, yeah, me have time for myself? That would be nice, but just not feasible at this point in time."

Celine stared at Melissa, making Melissa question what was up.

"You're a knockout, Mel. You could have your pick, yet you take care of everyone else and never focus on you. When was the last time you went out on a real date?"

Melissa chuckled. "Yeah, right, me have an actual relationship with a man. Didn't you see what happened with the last guy I dated?" Melissa finished stacking the cans of soup in the cupboard then took a seat on the chair at the table.

"You met him at the club, Mel. What type of individual did you think Bret would turn out to be?"

"Oh, I don't know, maybe a semi-decent guy. He was for the first two dates." Melissa played with the fringe on the lace tablecloth.

"He was decent for the first two minutes of the first and only date you went on with him. I remember the things he said to you, and I remember how his buddy Keith showed up at your aunt's apartment looking for you."

"Do you really have to bring this up right now?"

Melissa remembered the trouble she had gotten herself into. She thought Bret was going to be her knight in shining armor. Instead, he turned out to be a womanizer and a drug dealer to boot. The deliveries she went on when he offered her an easy job to make some fast money were a huge mistake on her part. She fell for Bret's good looks and charm, and she had shared her troubled life and her desperate need for cash to pay all the bills. There she was, learning the trade of delivering so-called "packages," which really contained drugs, for upscale clients for their parties. It only took a few days to learn the ins and outs of the business, and the money got her off the streets and into her current job at Charlie's club. It was an upscale joint with lots of money to be made.

"Hey, don't ponder over the bad stuff. You made it out of there, and Bret didn't turn you into a prostitute like he did Sally."

"You're right about that. But getting out from under his thumb was a whole different story. I swear, whenever he comes into the club now, he eyes me like he thinks he still has a hold on me. I wouldn't give him the time of day."

"He hasn't tried to ask you out again has he?"

Melissa's eyes widened as she thought about that scenario.

"Thank God, no. I couldn't even imagine. But I try to avoid him when he comes in. Some guys just don't know what the word 'no' means."

"Tell me about it. That asshole banker that was just here informed me that I can pay off my loan in other ways." Celine stared down at her hands as she said the words.

Melissa reached across the table and squeezed her hand.

"You didn't—"

"Hell no! My babies are in the other room, and I know men like that. My bills would suddenly increase, and I would be spreading my legs on a weekly basis instead of monthly. No thanks. We'll be just fine, thanks to you."

"I didn't do much," Melissa replied as she stared at her good friend Celine. Celine was an attractive woman with short, blonde hair and big, blue eyes. They had become friends shortly before Melissa's sister died.

"Bullshit you didn't. I'm getting a job. My bills are getting lower and lower thanks to you. You found me a babysitter I can trust and I feel confident leaving my kids with her while I'm at work. That means so much to me, Mel. Then you come around to check on me and still bring me groceries. You deserve the best, Mel. You deserve to start thinking about yourself a little."

Melissa sighed then smiled. She had done some crazy shit the last couple of years. Stuff that was better left unspoken about, but she never sacrificed her body.

"I give you credit, Celine. You could have made that asshole sign a contract that would be legal and binding with the right attorney if he welched on the deal."

"You see what I mean? You find a way to get around all the red tape and bring happiness and a better life to those in need. You've taken on an instant family with your sister's kids and your sick aunt. You helped get the soup kitchen back on its feet when the storage room was robbed of all the food. Holy shit! You're a fucking saint!" Celine teased, and Melissa started to laugh. She instantly thought about the numerous times she stole from a few rich, criminal businessmen and gave the money to the poor in the community. If Celine only knew.

A quick glance toward the microwave and she noticed the time. It was getting late, and tomorrow was a big day. As of right now she'd only get four hours of sleep before she had to get everyone up for school. Then she'd go back to bed for a few hours, and the kids would be home by three o'clock from school before she knew it. They would be going to the hospital to see her aunt and talk to the doctor.

"Well, I've got to go. I think they may be releasing Aunt Peggy from the hospital tomorrow. They ran a bunch of tests, and so far it looks like she's in remission."

"That's great. I am sure it has a lot to do with the treatment you got for her. The clinic nearly killed her."

"I know. I hate to think about all the other people that clinic failed."

"Oh no. Don't start worrying about the strangers again. You nearly wound up in jail, remember?"

"Of course I do. It was the scariest twenty-four hours of my life."

"Good old Charlie. He treats you like you're his daughter."

"He acted like I was his own daughter when he bailed me out of jail then reprimanded me."

They began walking across the living room to the front door.

"How did you get that money to pay for your aunt's surgery? And don't tell me by bartending at the club. That was big bucks to save her life. Oh, wait, you're not stripping are you? I heard that Lilly and some of the other girls get huge tips."

Melissa looked down at the rug. "Hell no! I could never do that. I am doing fine just working the bar. You would be surprised at how much I make in tips." She hoped her lie about the tips went unnoticed. She wasn't about to divulge any of her extracurricular activities. "Let's just say I came across an amazing opportunity and took advantage of it."

"Okay, don't tell me then. Whatever you did, it was well worth it."

Melissa said good-bye then exited the apartment.

Chapter 2

Vince and Frankie stood near the bar drinking their beers and talking about the drug bust their team engaged in tonight. It was intense for the average SWAT team officer but not for an Alpha were. It was difficult to get the scene out of his head as Vince recalled the setup. There were bullets flying all around them, drug dealers were armed with semiautomatic weapons, and they were secured inside a home armed with titanium doors as barricades.

"That's pretty fucking funny about that titanium door. How much you think that fucking thing cost?" Vince asked.

"Shit. I don't even know where the fuck you get titanium doors from as an average citizen," Frankie responded.

His brother laughed. "They weren't average citizens. They were drug dealers from Jamaica."

Frankie laughed. "You can buy a lot of expensive shit with 'fuck-you' money."

Just then Vince sniffed the air and smelled the female wolf as she approached the bar. His eyes roamed over her body from her six-inch, spiked red heels to her perky little breasts. She wasn't wearing any bra, or panties for that matter. The dress was skintight and matched her heels and her lipstick. Vince knew what she wanted, and with one glance toward his brother Frankie, it was on. They had seen her around this bar before, and she never dressed so provocatively.

"Hi," she whispered extra close to Vince's ear.

He took a slug from his beer and pretended he didn't notice her. She would need to know her place right off the bat. He knew what she was offering, but she didn't know what she was in for with him and Frankie.

Frankie stood up and towered over the female wolf by at least a foot. She was lanky, with long legs, thin arms, and a decent ass. Not their usual type, but she would do for tonight. They were both feeling rather stressed lately. Their other brothers were on edge as well, and there was no explanation in sight.

Frankie moved in behind the blonde and sniffed her neck. He knew immediately she was from Semora pack. It was a small, neutral wolf pack that had family scattered around the state of New York.

He placed his hands on her hips and gave a small thrust to her ass, letting his thick, hard cock press against the seam. She closed her eyes and leaned back against him.

Vince took control of the situation because it seemed they were drawing some attention from the crowd of humans around them.

"You, outside in thirty seconds," he stated then drank the rest of his beer before rising from the stool and leaving with his brother Frankie.

Vince looked at his military watch as they stood in the side parking lot of the building. She would have to use her wolf senses to know where to meet them. It was part of the game. The thrill of the chase.

"Did you see that fucking dress she had on?"

"I'm really not into this tonight," Vince stated, sounding annoyed with himself.

"What do you mean?"

"I'm just not—Bingo!" His watch beeped, indicating that the thirty seconds were up, and along came the blonde.

She wiggled her ass like she thought she was the hottest wolf in town. Her heels clanked on the blacktop with every step she took. In a flash, she lifted her dress from upper thigh to shoulders, up and over her head.

He was right. No fucking undergarments.

She pressed her small breasts against Vince's chest as she reached for his pants.

* * * *

Vince wasn't sure what the hell came over him, but he wasn't interested in getting any tonight. He had been fighting this sensation inside of him for weeks now. He started to think that there was more to his life than the SWAT team, the government job, and dedicating his entire life to the military.

He grabbed the blonde by her hands and stopped her.

"What's your problem?" she asked him. Then placed her hands on her hips.

She thought nothing about standing in the middle of the side parking lot completely naked in front of two wolves she didn't know. It bothered him. Wolves being sexual creatures was one thing, but putting out to any wolf sniffing was another. Vince didn't like women like this. He was annoyed now at his brother for provoking him.

* * * *

Frankie inhaled her scent, trying his hardest to keep interested. But one look at his brother Vince and all bets were off. His brother wasn't interested either. The smell of numerous colognes and both human and were-male scents made his stomach twist with disgust. She was nothing but a cheap whore, and that was it. He lost his desire as well. He was still a gentleman as he helped to locate her dress and tell her that they needed to go. Vince pretended that his phone vibrated as he followed Frankie's lead. The chick bought it, thinking they were really important as he helped her with her dress and thanked her for understanding. She smiled.

"You two can do me any time you want."

Her language bothered Frankie. Everything about her bothered him. As they watched her walk away and back into the bar, they walked silently to their truck. "We could have had sex with no strings attached and we both turned it down. What the hell?" Frankie stated, sounding annoyed.

* * * *

After making it halfway to their home, a thirty-minute drive into New Jersey and outside the city limits, Frankie spoke.

"What the fuck, Vince? That sucked."

"Why are you getting mad at me? You could have done your thing with her. I just wasn't attracted to her." Frankie glared at his brother. They shared the same brown eye color, the same six-foot-four-inch height, but their personalities were on complete opposite sides of the spectrum. Frankie loved having sex and could get it whenever he wanted it. He and his brothers were Alpha males, the finest specimen of their blood line. Even human women drooled when they caught sight of them. But Vince was more reserved. He was more like the wine-her-and-dine-her type of guy. Frankie loved pussy, and he didn't hide that fact, ever. He never left a woman unsatisfied, and neither did his other brothers, Logan, Sunny, and Jake.

"Why did you have to project your negativity in my direction?"

"I did no such thing. You're used to fucking any woman willing to open her thighs. I desire more in a woman before I have sex with her."

"Since when?"

"Fuck you!" Vince growled just as they approached the development where their house was.

Vince parked the truck and got out, slamming the door behind him.

As they entered the house, they heard the TV blaring and someone in the kitchen.

Vince looked around the room at his brothers. Logan was doing sit-ups in the living room and Sunny was watching TV and sipping a beer while Jake cooked up some midnight munchies in the kitchen.

"I'm hitting the shower," Vince stated in a nasty tone, walking out of the room.

"What the fuck is his problem?" Jake asked Frankie as he scrambled the eggs and removed the bacon from the frying pan. A pile of food sat on the counter waiting to be eaten.

Feeling frustrated, Frankie took a beer from the refrigerator then plopped down on the stool by the island in the kitchen.

"Nothing," he replied.

Jake sniffed the air then stared at Frankie and raised his eyebrows. He looked like the actor Dwayne Johnson when he did that. All the chicks went crazy over Jake. He was tall, muscular, and had brilliant colored brown eyes that were more wolf than human. Women loved that and were always complimenting Jake. He also carried himself very well. He enjoyed a fine wine, a gourmet meal, and more luxuries in life than the rest of them did. He knew how to cook, he was always suave and debonair, but if you pissed off his wolf, he would rip you to shreds. Frankie had seen it done before.

"Okay, so you two fuck the same chick and what, he wants to date her but can't because you fucked her?" Jake teased as he placed the food platters onto the island along with plates.

"What the fuck happened?" Sunny asked as he and Logan joined the conversation.

"It wasn't like that." Frankie ran and hand through his hair feeling the sexually frustration tighten every muscle in his body. The beer wasn't doing shit to easy his throbbing erection.

"Then tell us what happened, Frankie," Logan asked, but Frankie knew Logan meant business. As lead Alpha to their pack and SWAT team commander, he had the right to know everything that went on in their lives. Being their brother, he made sure they were protected.

This was his way of helping to ease a potential blowup between Frankie and Vince.

Frankie explained as he piled food onto his plate.

"So Vince wasn't in the mood but you wanted to have sex with the blonde anyway so you could get some pussy tonight? You should be thanking him. Vince is more sensitive when it comes to women," Sunny added as he piled food on his plate.

Frankie gave Sunny a dirty look. Sunny was built like a linebacker, big and bulky instead of a stealth ultimate fighter, lean and trim. Sunny and Logan were built like tanks. They were thick and their muscles were bulging everywhere. They had more than just definition. They looked pumped and ready at all times. Both wore their brown hair to shoulder length, and both were crazy wolves and men to deal with. Frankie, Vince, and Jake shared the same tempers, but they were each two hundred and fifty pounds, give or take a few pounds, and built like lean, muscular, ultimate fighters. They were pure muscle.

"Maybe this is something to be concerned about?" Logan asked as he finished eating his food in record time.

They were silent a moment. Logan spoke up first.

"He was kind of acting funny the last time we visited Samantha, Dustin, and the guys. He was envious that our cousins found their mate and she was with child."

"Don't even say it. I sure as shit am not going to settle down with one fucking woman and have sex with only her for the rest of my life. And kids? No fucking way. There is no woman out there with the strength, mental and physical tolerance, or the perfect body to make this dick give up free pussy," Frankie stated very seriously.

Sunny laughed.

"You have no clue, Frankie." Sunny shook his head.

"What?"

"Stop! There's no need to have this discussion anyway," Logan stated.

"It could happen. We each could find a mate or be like Dustin and the guys and share the same mate," Jake added to the conversation.

"All of us share one woman? Are you nuts? If I did find a mate, she would be so fucking occupied fucking me, she wouldn't have time to fuck any of you. She wouldn't need to."

Logan threw the rag at Frankie's head.

"Stop throwing around the *F* word so much. Just forget this conversation. No one knows if there is even a mate out there for any of us, never mind all of us. Besides, your shit isn't that good," Sunny teased.

"My dick is bigger than yours, Sunny," Frankie added.

"No fucking way," Sunny replied.

"Cut it out, we all know that I have the biggest dick," Jake stated very seriously as he cleared his plate.

They chuckled until Vince entered the room. He grabbed a beer and a plate of food. Everyone was silent.

He looked at his brothers and their sensitive expressions then at Frankie and shook his head.

"You fucking asshole, you told them?"

"Told us what?" Sunny asked, trying to act casual.

Frankie shook his head and took a seat at the table. His gut was bothering him since before the blonde at the bar came along. He really didn't want to engage in casual sex, but he couldn't admit that out loud. He had a reputation to uphold, and admitting that he wanted a relationship with the right woman could subject him to teasing his wolf wouldn't handle well. He swallowed hard, hoping the move submerged his true feelings.

"Well?" Vince persisted to get an answer from his brothers.

"Oh, you mean about the blonde with the pussy and ass made for fucking and how you got a limp dick?" Sunny teased, and all the brothers roared with laughter.

"I did not get a limp dick. Fuck, Frankie. You can be such an asshole. Just leave me alone. I'm not going out for drinks after work with you anymore. As a matter of fact, I'm done with bars for a while."

They continued to laugh until Jake spoke.

"Well, you can only stay away from them for a week. We have Alex's bachelor party at that place, Charlie's, downtown on Friday night."

Vince cringed just thinking about the place. It was supposedly an upscale strip club with great food and awesome entertainment.

"Just what I need."

Logan placed his hand on his brother's back in support.

"Don't worry, we'll have your back."

The brothers laughed.

* * * *

They cleaned up the kitchen and then went into the living room to turn on the news channel. Immediately, Jake saw the flashing lights and the media surrounding two sets of houses in a quiet neighborhood in Brooklyn. They listened as the reporter began to describe what was going on.

"It appears that it is going to be another case of an unsolved mystery. Police received a call forty minutes ago from an unidentifiable caller who stated that a large drug deal was about to go down in this quiet neighborhood. Unbeknownst to the police as they approached the area quietly and arrived prepared to catch the culprits of this large drug deal in action, the crooks became the victim. Instead, they found three irate alleged drug dealers, ripped off by a crook they didn't know and couldn't identify."

The men listened as the reporter spoke and then tried to get a statement from one of the men arrested.

"Look at those assholes. They deserve to get busted and go to jail," Jake stated, and his brothers agreed.

"Sir, can you give us a statement, please? What happened?" the reporter asked one of the patrol sergeants.

"It appears that the drug dealers were ripped off. A deal went down. The other party who paid an unknown amount of money for the drugs were arrested two blocks from here. These three morons were robbed by someone in a black mask. They held them by gunpoint and stole the cash."

"Any ideas who the suspect who robbed the men is, and whether or not they planned this attack with the intent to get the drugs off of the streets?"

"No. But if I did, I would shake their hand. We found a street value of more than sixty thousand dollars worth of cocaine on those guys. That's a lot of drugs."

"Are you condoning the behavior, Sergeant?" The reporter asked.

"Hell no. A crime is a crime, but this is a big bust. These guys are wanted for numerous crimes. There's a felony warrant out for one of the guys at the scene two blocks over. A great night for the NYPD."

With that the sergeant walked away.

"That's incredible. I would like to think that someone good stole the money. Maybe a citizen fed up with the system and the way some of these neighborhoods are being overpowered by drug dealers," Frankie stated.

"Two wrongs don't make a right, brother. A crime is a crime even if it's the criminals getting ripped off," Vince added, sounding firm.

"Still, could you imagine if there was a modern day Robin Hood out there? Maybe they're stealing from the wealthy drug-dealing criminals and giving back to the poor? That's my kind of story," Frankie replied.

"Whatever. I'm going to bed," Sunny mumbled then walked out of the room. Soon after, the others called it a night as well. But Frankie stared at the television screen as the news continued. He couldn't help but fantasize about the possibility of a modern-day do-gooder. He thought about the criminals he and his brothers had fought over the years. He thought about the secret government jobs and the corruption even in political office. He shook his head.

"No way could it be true," he stated to an empty room, then clicked off the television and went to bed.

Chapter 3

Melissa let the hot water soothe her muscles. Tonight's hit was a close call. She had no idea that three men were going to show up and not just one of Carlos's guys. This had to be one of her last hits. Aunt Peggy was coming home tomorrow now that Melissa had the last thirty grand for the medical bills. Thank god she was able to sweet-talk to the nice old doctor and tell him she worked for cash and didn't have any credit cards. Her sister had only a small amount of money set aside for the kids in their own savings account. Melissa had added more, and now those savings accounts were looking decent, and the money had to remain in the account for their education. Sarah and Mike were so in love. They were making it. They were surviving on their own with great jobs and a promising future until that night. Melissa still couldn't believe that they were caught in the middle of a drug war and drive-by shooting that left Brandon, Lea, and Tommy with no parents and a sickly great-aunt. If not for Melissa, they would have wound up in foster care, separated and alone.

It had been a sacrifice. Melissa thought about the time she spent working as a secretary for the district attorney's office. She was taking college courses and was going to pursue her law degree when the accident happened. Her whole world changed, and one look into her niece and nephews' eyes and she knew she was their only hope. She grew up practically on the streets, and she and her sister got out together and succeeded. It fucking sucked that her sister and husband died. There wasn't enough money for their house, for their bills, or for the funeral. Then Aunt Peggy got sick and was diagnosed with cancer on top of it all. Melissa felt the tears sting her eyes. Things were better now. She was forced to make some unethical choices, but so far she was in the clear, and at least she didn't have to whore out her body for money. She had contemplated doing that and came close, but something stopped her.

Turning the water off, she stepped out of the shower, towel dried her hair, and then wrapped a towel around her waist.

Glancing in the mirror, she swallowed hard.

That was a close one tonight. I nearly lost it all. She walked into the bedroom.

She turned on the television, making sure the volume was low so she wouldn't wake the kids. Staring at the screen, she saw the reporters talking about the hit on the drug dealers. The media was having a ball with this.

The near-death experience had shined some reality on her nighttime excursions. When the drug dealer shot the semiautomatic gun around the air, causing the bullets to come too close for comfort to her, she was relieved that she wasn't hit. She got the gun away, held them at gunpoint, and took the eighty grand. A big "thank-you" to Chu for teaching her some amazing moves in self-defense. Too bad she couldn't call him. He was Bret's personal bodyguard.

Melissa needed to stop pondering over the what-ifs and be grateful she had the money. It had to be done. Aunt Peggy wouldn't be released until the bills were partially paid. The longer she stayed there, the higher the bill. The financial secretary appeared shocked when Melissa handed over thirty thousand in cash and to her and asked for a receipt.

People had no heart anymore. They didn't empathize with the needy at all. It was sad. The drug dealers were killing kids and ruining society while the good, innocent people suffered and lived in shelters, afraid to sleep. Not that she was contemplating becoming some sort of vigilante. She wasn't committing murder or anything like that. She was just stealing money from thieves who stole money from other thieves and junkies who needed to support their addictions. She wasn't stealing from the needy, the working class, or anyone just trying to make ends meet. She was improvising, overcoming, and adapting to the environment she lived with the cards she was dealt. If she led a straight and narrow life, she would be working the corner, her niece and nephews would be separated and in foster care, and her aunt would be dead. It was a no-brainer as far as she was concerned. Plus there were other people in this building who needed help and were struggling to survive just like Melissa and her own family. Someone had to do something. The neighbors didn't ask questions. They just thanked her and thanked her over and over again every time she delivered groceries, baby formula, clothing, or cash for rents.

But tonight had been a close call. Perhaps this would be her last hit on the bad guys.

* * * *

Melissa spoke to Charlie on her cell phone as she waited for the nurse to finish getting her aunt ready to leave. Charlie had become more than a boss over the past year. She considered him a close friend.

"I'm so happy your aunt is getting better. It's great that she can go back home with you and the kids. Call me if you need anything," Charlie stated.

"I will, Charlie. Thanks a bunch," she replied then said goodbye before closing up the phone.

Melissa helped her Aunt Peggy into the wheelchair. She looked amazing, considering she had surgery only a week before. The preliminary tests showed that the doctors had gotten all the cancer. They would run more tests and have her come back for blood work in a week or so.

"Oh, Aunt Peggy, we're so glad that you're coming back home," Lea stated as she hugged her aunt. Melissa thought that Lea, her sister's twelve-year-old daughter, looked just like Sarah. She had long, thick brown hair and green eyes just like her mother. She was very smart in school, and she loved playing sports. Melissa would ensure that Lea had a chance at success in life. She loved her as if she were her own child. Lea's brothers Brandon and Tommy gave Aunt Peggy hugs next. They were great kids. Brandon was adorable with big, bright brown eyes and dimples in his cheeks. A typical eight-year-old, he talked nonstop and was always making some sort of noise whether it was gunfire or racecar driving. Even his baby brother Tommy tried to make the noises, too. Melissa took Tommy's hand and smiled at the scene. They would all be home, there were no more hospital bills to pay, and they could work on getting back into a normal routine again.

They all gathered around Aunt Peggy and made their way down the hallway. As they approached the nurses' station, they saw shocked expressions and what Melissa could only describe as sadness on their faces.

"What's going on?" Brandon asked. For an eight-year-old he was very mature. He was handsome like Sarah's husband and very smart in school.

Some older nurse Melissa recognized placed her hand on his shoulder as she spoke.

"It seems that the fundraiser set up to help financially support the children's burn unit outreach program has been robbed."

"What?" Brandon and Lea both asked. They explained to Melissa that the program started a month ago and they raised over ten thousand dollars. It was a program to help children and their families who were victims of burns from fires or chemicals. She remembered them talking about it and how both Lea and Brandon took money from their piggy banks and added it to the donation box.

A few feet away, some children from the burn unit sat crying as nurses and adults tried consoling them. It was very disheartening to witness.

"That's terrible," Aunt Peggy added then shook her head.

"There's no way we can make back that money. I guess we can hope that people hear this latest, televised broadcast and donate again," the nurse stated then walked away.

* * * *

The kids were sad on the way home to the apartment. Even Aunt Peggy was bummed about the robbery. It gave Melissa an idea as she got everyone inside.

When they arrived home, their neighbor Alice talked with Peggy and promised to help out watching her and checking on her throughout the day. Alice offered to help put the kids on the bus and get Tommy to the preschool program he attended, but Melissa declined. That's why she had been thrilled with the bartending job. It kept her mornings and afternoons free so she could make the kids breakfast, get them on the bus, go to their school functions, and also take care of Tommy. He was just a baby really, and it had been tough to explain to him why Mommy and Daddy never came back home.

Melissa walked into the children's bedroom to tuck them in for the night. She saw Brandon emptying out his piggy bank and counting money.

He looked rather upset.

"What's wrong, Brandon?" she whispered as she took a seat beside him on the rug.

"I only have three dollars and twenty-five cents. That's not going to make a difference for the kids at the hospital." He looked so sad her heart ached. He was such a kind soul. He was always worried about everyone else. It had been tough getting him to talk about his loss and his emotions. But somehow he finally warmed up to Melissa and had been in better spirits.

Melissa placed her arm over his shoulder. "It will all work out, Brandon. You'll see."

"But how, Aunt Melissa? How can you be sure when someone so bad, so evil took all that money from those sick kids?"

"I just have a feeling, Brandon."

Brandon stood up and plopped down on his bed with his arms crossed in front of his chest.

Melissa stood up and joined him.

"There are more bad people out there than good people."

Melissa felt his upset and tried to encourage him.

"There are more good people out there than you think, Brandon. As a matter of fact, I bet right now, someone is gathering up that ten thousand dollars and preparing to give it to the hospital for those children," she stated as she helped him to lie down then covered his body with the sheets and comforter.

"Really?" he asked, sounding hopeful.

"Really. Now, go to sleep. You have school tomorrow, and I have to run out for a little bit. Lea knows I'll be gone for a bit, but Alice is home next door in case there's an emergency, okay."

"Okay," he stated then reached out and hugged Melissa's neck.

"I love you, Aunt Mel."

"I love you, too, squirt. Now get to sleep," she whispered as she left the room with tears in her eyes.

It was a peaceful night, and once everyone settled down and was fast asleep, Melissa headed out to the hospital.

* * * *

The following day Melissa got up early and made homemade pancakes and lots of bacon for breakfast. Her aunt had a great night's sleep now that she was back in her own bed. In a few weeks she would be as good as new.

"So, how is the job going?" her aunt asked as Melissa piled the pancakes onto the ceramic dish.

"It's going well."

"And the studying for the exam?"

"Ahhh...not so well. I've been real busy."

"Well, in a few weeks you can totally focus on your studies, and I will be well enough to care for the kids."

"Don't rush it, Aunt Peggy. We'll be okay."

"Don't be silly. You need time to study for the bar exam and work on achieving your dream. Being a bartender won't look good on your résumé," she added, showing her disapproval of Melissa's line of work. Thank God she didn't know that Melissa contemplated stripping, never mind the hits.

Lea woke up and was watching TV with Brandon as she helped baby Tommy get dressed for the day.

"Hey, Aunt Peggy, Aunt Mel, check this out," Lea yelled.

"Oh my God, that is awesome!" Brandon screamed and then started dancing around the room.

Melissa and her aunt looked at the TV from the kitchen and heard the news report. Brandon raised the volume so they could hear the reporter.

"It appears that a miracle has taken place here at St. Mary's Presbyterian Hospital. Yesterday we reported the sad and shocking news that ten thousand dollars had been stolen from the children's burn unit fundraiser. It was appalling and upsetting, but it seems that the children's prayers were answered. This morning Dr. Monogy found an envelope of money inside of the donation box. It was labeled to be used for the burn unit fund."

"Dr. Monogy, what did you think when you found this envelope?" the reporter asked the doctor he was interviewing.

"I was so excited and shocked that there was someone out there, a Good Samaritan ready to help our children."

"I understand that ten thousand dollars was stolen. How much did the envelope contain?"

"Twenty thousand!" he exclaimed.

"Twenty thousand dollars? That is double of what you had to begin with. Who do you think did this?" the reporter asked.

"I have my theories, and so does some of the hospital staff," he stated with a wink.

Melissa felt her heart pound in her chest.

"And what theory is that?" the female reporter asked.

"I think we'll keep it to ourselves. But if you're out there and listening to this report, we thank you from the bottom of our hearts. The children and their families thank you, too," the doctor stated into the camera.

* * * *

The children were all wired with excitement as Brandon grabbed Melissa's hands and started dancing around the living room. Melissa was feeling a bit nervous about what the doctor said about his suspicions, but there was no way he knew it was her. As she danced with Brandon, Lea, and Tommy, enjoying their happiness and smiling faces, she knew it had been worth the risk. Plus, the money she had gotten off the drug dealers was more than she had thought. After paying off some of the tenants' rents for the next six months and getting gift cards for groceries for them, she was still in decent shape with twenty thousand dollars left over. Today she would add money to the kids' savings accounts.

She made them settle down to eat breakfast, and afterwards they were all still excited, even as they got ready for school. She got them on the bus outside of the apartment then headed upstairs to help her aunt and take care of Tommy.

Melissa settled her aunt down on the couch before listening to her messages on the answering machine. Tommy remained watching children's shows and drawing on his drawing pad.

More bad news. The babysitter was sick and couldn't watch the kids Friday, Saturday, or Sunday. Melissa had to work. There was a big party Friday night and she had to bartend. Just then her cell phone rang. *Celine.*

"Hey, how did everything work out? Is Aunt Peggy settled back in yet?" Celine asked. Her chipper mood could be felt through the phone. Melissa laughed.

"Yes, she's doing great."

"You sound funny. Is everything all right?"

"My babysitter just bailed on me for this whole weekend. I have a party to do Friday, and I'm scheduled to work Saturday and Sunday."

"I can come over if your aunt won't mind another three kids. Plus they adore Lea. She is so mature and such a good babysitter. She may be able to do that for money in a couple of years."

"Don't you have to work?"

"Nope. I worked all week. Carl gave me off this weekend. I figured I would clean the apartment and maybe take the kids to the park with Brandon and Tommy if that was okay with you."

"Carl, huh? Since when did you start calling Mr. Baker Carl?"

"Since he took me out for coffee and dessert after work Monday night." Celine giggled.

"Oh no. You'd better be careful. If things don't work out, you'll lose that job."

"Charlie didn't fire you after you broke things off with Bret."

"Bret's a complete asshole, and Charlie knows it. Jobs aren't coming around easy these days. I would hate for you to lose it when you're catching up with all the bills."

"He owns the club with him. Isn't he like a partner or something?"

Melissa laughed to herself. Celine knew how to run a conversation and steer it in her direction.

"Like, not even a quarter of a partner."

"Oh well, I'll be careful. What time do you need me Friday?"

"Five o'clock okay?"

"Sure. Warn Aunt Peggy about my babies. They have been a handful lately. I pass out the second my head hits the pillow at night."

"No worries, Celine. Besides, Lea will be here to help. She loves Zack, Kelly, and Zoey."

"Great. I will see you on Friday. Oh, I almost forgot."

"Forgot what?"

"I was thinking."

"Oh, shit! Not a good thing at all."

"Cut it out, Mel, and hear what I have to say. I know this guy Paul."

"Oh no! You are not trying to set me up with someone are you?"

"No, Mel. I was just going to tell you that this guy Paul said that he knows you. Apparently he worked with your brother-in-law for a few years in the narcotics division. He and I got to talking at the party I hosted last night, at the gig you got me. Anyway, he said he was in desperate need of a bartender for this new restaurant. It has a private room for meetings or something and they have their own bar there. His friend opened it about a year ago. I told him I don't know how to tend bar but that my best friend bartends. He said that the position requires confidentiality. Apparently some heavy stuff is discussed in this bar."

"Sounds illegal to me," Melissa replied as she looked over the bowl of fresh fruit and debated about having a banana.

"He said there's all cops involved and in tips alone you could make a few grand a night. Man, I wish I knew how to bartend."

"A few grand! What the hell kind of outfit do I have to wear, and do I have to take it off in front of the patrons or something?"

"No! Paul said that the outfit is skimpy. All the waitstaff and bartenders wear them. Besides, you've worked the bar at Stiletto's, and that's a strip club."

"Oh, great! Throw that in my face, too. I have never stripped before just bartended private parties. I'll have you know that the only reason I did those few private parties in the back room was because of Marcy and her kids, Joyce and her three kids, as well as Turner, Margaret, and Barbara. If I hadn't made that twenty grand, working my rear off for that entire weekend, they would have been tossed out onto the streets and their kids would be in foster care, separated from their families. No freaking way would I have let that happen."

"I know, I know, I wasn't throwing it in your face. You've helped so many people in this neighborhood, Mel. I know you have your own nieces and nephews to worry about and your sick aunt. This job could bring some big money, and you wouldn't have to show off that fabulous body of yours in some too tight T-shirt for a bunch of perverted men. It would be better, that's all I'm saying. Then when you take the bar exam and pass, you could get a regular job and maybe defend people like me in court who get ripped off by the scumbags of society."

Melissa sighed.

"Okay, give me the number. I'll check it out."

"Yeah!" Celine exclaimed before she hung up the phone.

* * * *

Thirty minutes later, as Melissa cleaned the apartment and restocked the pantry for the weekend, her cell phone rang. She didn't recognize the number but answered it anyway.

"Hello, is Melissa there?" the person asked, and she didn't recognize the male voice.

"Who is this?"

"Is this Melissa?"

She was getting annoyed.

"Who is this?"

"Um...I'm looking for Melissa. I'm a friend of Celine's, and I used to know Melissa's brother-in-law Mike."

Oh crap.

"I'm so sorry, this is Melissa. I didn't recognize your voice, and you didn't identify yourself."

"No problem. It's my fault. I'm in a bit of a rush today preparing the restaurant for the crowd Saturday. Celine said you were interested in the position."

"I may be. I kind of work at another place right now."

"I know she told me. Charlie's, right? I've known him for years. This won't interfere with your schedule. It wouldn't be all the time, or it could be if you like working for me. It's up to you. The thing is, I need someone for Saturday night."

"I'm sorry I'm working Saturday at Charlie's."

"I'm sure he can find someone to cover your shift. I promise it will be worth it. Celine swears by your abilities as a bartender."

Melissa released a sigh. "Did Celine also swear by my body for this mysterious outfit I need to wear?"

He chuckled, but it sounded kind of nice.

"It's really not a mysterious outfit. It's a short black miniskirt, high heels, and a very unique tip-getting kind of top."

"Oh, really? Like the kind where my boobs are about to pour into the drinks along with the liquor?"

He laughed again, and his chuckle was appealing. Oh my god, she was wondering what this Paul looked like.

"Listen, come by today and check it out. If you don't like it, then don't take the job. I'll be here for the next two hours. Do you know where we're located?"

"Yes, I do. Okay, I'll be there in thirty minutes."

She hung up the phone and wondered if she made a huge mistake. She prepared Tommy's snack for nursery school, cleaned up, changed into a better outfit, then headed out to drop Tommy off and meet this Paul guy.

Chapter 4

"What do you mean you can't work tomorrow night? I need you," Charlie stated as Melissa fixed her lip gloss and adjusted her boobs in the three-sizes-too-small tank top she was forced to wear. The outfit at Paul's wasn't half as bad. It was just that the tank top literally showed off her whole stomach. The fact that her belly was pierced made for more tips, too. Guys liked belly rings. The outfit turned out to be not as bad as she feared. It was kind of cute, just like Paul, and it was black and purple.

"I have another gig, and the money's really good. You know I need to take care of the family."

"Shit, Mel! How much they paying you, and please tell me you're not gonna leave here without warning me."

Melissa smiled and then patted Charlie's arm.

"I wouldn't do that."

"Good. Now, are we all set for your number at ten? I can't believe that Lilly did this to me."

"She got sick, Charlie. It happens." Melissa fidgeted with the tie on the back of her apron. She was a nervous wreck since Charlie begged her to take Lilly's place tonight. There was a huge bachelor party coming in and they expected to see Lola Lamore. Lilly owed her big time, too.

"I need you to pull this off, Mel. I got her wig, a lot of makeup, and everything you requested."

"Yeah, yeah, yeah. Just be ready to give me a huge bonus for going onstage. I had promised myself I would never do this. So if you tell a soul, I'm going to kill you."

"I promise that your secret will stay with me. You did this once before you know?"

"I was a background singer for the fifties night a year ago. It doesn't compare to dancing in front of a huge crowd and a bachelor party no less. My nerves are getting the best of me and I feel like I'm going to vomit. Now let me get back to the bar. It's getting crowded and Jerry looks nervous."

Charlie looked toward the bar, and he smiled. Jerry, the other bartender couldn't keep up with the drinks.

* * * *

Melissa started taking drink orders, and the guys loaded up the barstools. They were all gawking at her and flirting like mad. She did the same and continued flirting as her tip jar filled up to the rim.

Around nine o'clock, a large crowd of men showed up for the bachelor party. One look in that direction and she could tell that they were cops. The bachelor looked like he knew his way around a whiskey bottle and a woman's body as his friends paid for lap dance after lap dance. The bachelor had a lot of money on him.

The sound of laughter caught her attention as five men gathered around the bar, making the current eight men who were already there leave immediately. It was as if these five men were important. Melissa froze in place the moment her eyes caught sight of them. Talk about huge, gorgeous men. These guys were eye candy and a half with their tight T-shirts, big muscles, and nice smiles. In an instant her nipples hardened and other dormant body parts awoke. *Shit!*

Things like this didn't happen to her, so she ignored her gut instincts and walked toward them.

"Hey, fellas, can I get you something to drink?" she asked as she leaned over the counter to wipe it down and place five drink coasters on the shiny wood.

"Yeah, sweetheart, we'll take five beers," one big guy with brown hair to his shoulders stated. His hair was shiny and wild looking. It fell to his shoulders and gave him an animalistic kind of look. Tamable he wasn't, so she looked at the other guy. He appeared just as wild as the first guy. Except this one had gorgeous brown eyes that appeared to sparkle in the low lit room instead of look dull. Oh well, wild and untamable was not a good combination for her unless she was into one-night stands. Arms like theirs around someone her petite size would feel amazing, she was certain. She walked away and began to fill their order.

* * * *

Logan was the first to speak to the bartender and place the order. Man, did she have a nice rack on her and an ass made for holding on to. He inhaled as she set the coasters down and when she turned to walk away. Her scent interested him, but there was a combination of perfume and numerous colognes around him. He stared at her as she made the beers. He watched as men flirted with her and she flirted back. She had an adorable smile and looked kind of sweet and innocent. But with a body like hers, she most likely was experienced. If not, he would love to break her in. It had been a while since a woman interested him and especially one that looked at him with big brown doe eyes and as if he was just another guy.

* * * *

"Hey, what's up with you?" Vince asked Logan as he followed his line of sight. He, too, focused on the brunette. She had a great set of tits on her that made the word *Charlie* spread out across the front. The waitress taking orders had a smaller set of breasts on her, and the name *Charlie* covered her chest from rib to rib. This bartender was hot.

She returned, smiling wide as she clutched three cold mugs of beer in one hand and two in the other. The tank top showed off the definition in her upper arms. She definitely liked to work out.

"There you go, sweetie," she stated, taking the fifty-dollar bill from Logan. That's when they caught her scent.

Vince nearly growled, but Logan grabbed his arm and smiled at the bartender.

"Keep the change, honey. We'll be here all night," he told her, and she winked at him. Instantly Vince's cock hardened and pressed against his zipper.

"I don't fucking believe this!" Vince stated through their link.

"Neither do I. She's fucking incredible," Logan added.

"Who's incredible?" Sunny asked, joining them.

"Jake, Frankie, get over here," Logan demanded, and immediately they gathered around Logan.

"Check out the bartender," Vince stated, and his brothers watched as the bartender served some patrons at the other end.

"Yeah, she's hot," Frankie added.

"Get her to come back down here and you'll know what Vince and I mean," Logan stated firmly.

Frankie whistled loudly, and immediately the bartender turned toward them. She was gorgeous. She appeared to look annoyed at the fact that Frankie whistled at her, but quickly she gave that sexy smile and wiggled her way toward them.

* * * *

Melissa couldn't believe that one of those big guys whistled at her like a dog. What the hell. Obviously good looks went only so far.

She approached them, and all five were staring at her. She had an uneasy feeling in the pit of her stomach. These guys were way bigger than most cops she had seen around. They towered over everyone currently in the club tonight. She swallowed the feeling of intimidation and put on her best smile.

"What can I do for you, darling?" she asked just as the other bartender asked her a question. She turned her head, causing her ponytail to whip in front of her then back around.

When she turned to see what the guy wanted, he had a look of pure lust in his eyes. It was amazing and it gave her the chills. "What can I get you, honey?" she asked again as she stared into a gorgeous set of brown eyes. He didn't answer her, so she looked toward the big guy with the brown hair to his shoulders.

"He'll take another beer, doll."

Melissa got him another beer then continued to serve the other patrons. The five guys remained crowded around the bar asking her for beers or shots, never leaving the spot. They were tipping well, so she really didn't care. They engaged her in small talk and seemed really nice.

She absorbed their similar good looks and identical eye color. That's when it hit her.

"Are you guys brothers?" she asked, but the music was too loud as the strippers took the stage and the bachelor had a front-row seat.

"What?" the one guy with the short brown hair and a solid, muscular body asked. He looked like he had been in the military.

She leaned over the bar, and the guy leaned over closer. Their heads nearly bumped, and they both laughed. Up close he was even more handsome. There was a look in his eyes that did a number on her insides. She wanted to ask his name, but then he would think she was interested. So far they hadn't asked her name yet.

"I asked if you all were brothers."

He held her gaze and inhaled as if he smelled her.

It should have felt creepy, but instead, her body seemed to react in its own way. She felt the sudden moisture against her folds. *Holy fuck!* This guy was so hot he could make her come just by whispering to her.

"Yes, we are," the other guy answered, and she wondered how the hell he heard her when he was so far away. She had a funny feeling in her stomach and quickly looked toward the clock on the wall. She had to get ready for her set, and it took time to do the makeup and attach the wig. She'd better disguise herself well or one of these brothers was going to grope her on the stage. The thought caused a tingling in her belly.

* * * *

Logan watched as the bartender walked toward the end of the bar and spoke with another bartender.

"What do we do?" Frankie asked.

"Nothing we can do without scaring her," Logan stated.

"How can you be so fucking calm when we just found our fucking mate?" Vince asked.

"Because we know she works here and she's not going anywhere?" Logan replied, and Frankie looked down the bar for her.

"We should have grabbed her when we could have. She's gone," he replied, sounding annoyed, and his brothers all searched the bar for her.

"Fuck!" Sunny exclaimed.

"Don't panic. She has to be around here somewhere. Do what we do best and investigate," Logan added, and they all agreed to find out anything they could about the bartender.

* * * *

Logan and Vince were caught up in questioning Charlie, the owner of the place, when suddenly the main strip act was about to begin. Logan and his brothers joined the rest of the crowd as everyone pushed for a front row seat.

"I love you, Charlie!" the bachelor, Alex, exclaimed as he moved as close as he could to the stage.

"What the fuck is the big deal?" Frankie asked Alex's partner and fellow cop, Ken.

"This dancer is special. She only performs once a month, or maybe two or three months could pass without her performing. The rumor is she's in the witness protection program."

"What?" Frankie asked then chuckled.

"I've got to see this."

"I'm telling you, Frankie, once you get a load of the body on this blonde, you will be searching for a woman just like her and coming back here week after week."

"She's that fucking hot?" Frankie asked, and his buddy nodded.

The lights lowered, leaving a slight dim over the stage and nowhere else.

The announcer's voice echoed over the loudspeaker.

"Gentlemen, Stiletto's is honored to have a special guest this evening in honor of one of our loyal patrons, Officer Alex." The crowd of men cheered and screamed as Alex sat holding the sides of his seat with anticipation. The sound of a slow drum beating in the background added to the anticipation of the announcement.

"Stiletto's is proud to introduce for your ultimate pleasure this evening, in one of her rare appearances, Miss Lola Lamore!"

The audience roared with excitement as the drum roll began and instantly a bright light shined on Miss Lola from the breasts down.

"Holy fuck!" Frankie exclaimed and his brothers added similar comments.

They wanted closer and now regretted not moving in while they had a chance, but they were looking for their mate.

* * * *

Logan gave up trying to see around the crowded, dark club and instead focused on the voluptuous blonde on stage. She wore six-inch stilettos and had the most perfect set of toned, muscular legs he'd ever seen on a woman. The fire-engine red nightie and a sequin mask that only covered her eyes left just enough to the imagination. She was built like a sex goddess. The sheer nightie was decorated with sequins and light, fluffy fur on the edges and matched the mask. She stood with her hands on her curvy hips then bent forward as the music began. From there on out, Logan was in a daze.

"My dick is so hard right now, I think I'm gonna come in my fucking pants," Frankie stated through their link.

The stripper reached for the pole, pressing her satin-covered pussy against it as she arched backwards in a very interesting and precarious-looking position without hesitation and with perfection. Her large breasts moved past the material, revealing just a touch of her deeper colored areola and more sequins.

"I just came in my fucking pants," Sunny moaned.

The stripper slowly pumped up and down against the pole with one hand while she sucked and licked her finger as if she were sucking cock.

The crowd of men roared louder. As the beat of the music picked up, the stripper wiggled and strutted around the edge of the dance floor, letting men stuff bills in the elastic of her tiny string panties as well as the cleavage of her sexy bra. Logan noticed that the stripper covered more of her body than most but the men didn't seem to mind. Him included.

She then made her way near the bachelor, who was so excited, he nearly climbed up on stage. The bouncer was going to stop him, but the blonde took complete control of the situation, knowing it was the guy's bachelor party.

"I say if Alex tries something, we save the blonde and take her to her dressing room in the back," Jake suggested, and his brothers chuckled as they watched the scene unfold.

She kept him in control by grabbing a fistful of his hair and yanking him up onto the stage but making Alex remain on his knees. The crowd of men roared louder as she wiggled around him, barely touching his body yet eliciting moans and sexual innuendos from both Alex and the crowd.

When she stopped in front of Alex with her back facing him then bent forward, displaying her ass in his face, Alex roared. But he didn't touch her. It was as if he was afraid to do it, and she was too hot for him to handle.

"Touch her!" the crowd yelled.

"Smack that ass!" they cheered, but he didn't do it. Instead, the blonde slapped herself on the ass cheek then gave a light push to Alex's chest, causing him to fall to the stage floor on his back.

The music continued as she did a sexy dance over his face and body. At the end she kissed her finger then touched it to his lip and chin. She was about to move away and the song seemed like it was ending when Alex grabbed her wrist.

"Wait," he begged of her then reached into his pocket and pulled out a wad of hundred-dollar bills. He began to tuck them into her waist then into her cleavage. He ran out of room but still had bills in his hand. She tilted her chin forward with her mouth open and took them from him with her teeth.

The whistles and grunts filled the air, and slowly she began to rise up and down as if she was dry-humping him. She seductively rubbed her hands up over her breasts then over the small knot that kept her little red nightie together. She removed the garment then wrapped it around Alex's neck as a memento. Her breasts were completely exposed except for her red sequin-covered nipples. Her abs looked tight and defined, and the ruby-red stone in her belly button accentuated her curves. Rising, she sashayed away, stopping here and there for more patrons to hand her money. As she exited the stage, the crowd clapped and whistled, asking for more and for the blonde to come back again.

* * * *

"I've never seen anything like that in my life," Vince stated to Logan as they cringed from the loud screams.

"Me either. She was fucking hot. The other women don't have a body like hers."

"That's why she's so special, Commander. She doesn't perform often, and only for special occasions or surprise events. Charlie hooked up Alex because he's good friends with Alex's cousin," Dave Flynn, Alex's Lieutenant, stated to Logan and Vince.

They watched as Alex received slaps on his back and comments about the performance on stage.

Logan and Vince were listening as he walked by them smiling and laughing. Suddenly, Logan stopped Alex and grabbed him. He inhaled as Vince did the same.

"What's up?" Alex asked, sounding drunk.

"Nothing. Congratulations!" Vince said then pulled Logan's hands off of Alex's shirt. Frankie, Jake, and Sunny joined them.

"That stripper was amazing, and what a fucking body. Man, I wish I could find me a piece of ass like that to take home. I'd never let her out of my bed," Sunny said.

"What's wrong with him?" Jake asked Vince.

"The stripper? She's our mate," he stated, and their low growls filled the immediate space.

Frankie grabbed Logan's shirt. "What are you fucking saying?"

"Go smell Alex right now. Our mate's scent is all over his fucking clothes," he stated through clenched teeth.

"Let's go find her," Sunny growled then looked around the room like a wild animal. Vince pulled Logan and Sunny closer.

"We can't do that. How the fuck are we going to explain that we know the stripper and the bartender are the same person?"

"We don't have to explain shit. She's done working here. She's done on that fucking stage. And if I see another man touch her I'm going to rip his fucking throat out."

"Calm down, Logan. We need to think about this."

They all looked at Jake.

"Did you have your eyes covered when our mate was up there stripping? She's ours, no one else's, Jake. This ends now!" Frankie growled then headed through the crowd. His brothers had no other choice but to follow him.

* * * *

"That was fantastic, Mel! My God, that crowd is still cheering for more. I think that was our best performance yet," Charlie stated as Melissa removed the money from her underwear and cleavage. The long silk robe hung open as she did it.

"Don't get any ideas, Charlie. That was probably my last performance."

"No! Oh, please, you can't be serious? Look at the money you just made."

She stared at him through the mirror.

"I don't like doing it. You know that, Charlie, so why are you pushing this?"

"How are you going to maintain paying the bills and helping all those people you are financially supporting?"

She released a sigh.

"I'll figure it out, Charlie. With Aunt Peggy out of the hospital and most of the bills paid, I'm in better shape. Celine has that job and a babysitter, and the others are all working now and supporting their own families. I need to worry about the kids."

* * * *

Frankie heard the whole conversation, and so did his brothers. They waited for Charlie to leave the room, and when he did, they told him they needed to see Lola.

"Sorry, guys, she's off-limits." He refused then tried to get them to go back into the hallway.

"It's important, Charlie, and you know we're not here to hurt her," Logan added.

"I can't. She's a good friend, and despite what you just saw out there, she's shy and really a great person. I think of her like a daughter. Lola doesn't see anyone offstage."

They were silent a moment. They really didn't want to force their way in there.

"How about Mel? Would she be interested in seeing us?" Vince asked, remembering that the other bartender told him that was the female bartender's name.

Charlie's eyes widened. "What are you talking about?"

"We know that Lola and Melissa are the same person."

"No one knows that. She's kept it a secret for a reason. She has kids, a family to support, and bills for her sick aunt. Please, guys," Charlie begged.

Logan touched his arm.

"We're not going to hurt her. She's important to us, Charlie. She's our mate," he stated then showed his wolf eyes to Charlie.

* * * *

Charlie wasn't completely shocked that these men were weres. He knew wolves existed and most kept their identities to themselves. He had a cousin who was mated to a wolf, so he knew the intensity of finding a mate. Maybe this was Mel's chance at happiness.

"I understand, but she might not. She's independent, and she's tougher than nails, especially when it comes to men. Tread carefully, guys. I'll give you some time with her, but she really is needed behind the bar. Plus she has a private party in the back room tonight."

With that, Charlie left the room.

* * * *

Melissa felt her heart beating rapidly in her chest. It had been exhilarating and exciting to be up on stage and dance like that. Of course she was more confident because of the wig and makeup. She could never do that on a regular basis. Her nerves would be shot, and she didn't like the way men looked at her as if they had every right to touch her.

As she danced for Alex, she noticed the brothers that were keeping her entertained all night at the bar. The look in the one big guy's eyes burned her insides. She never felt anything like that in her life. Then, when she was squatting over Alex, pretending to fuck him with her clothes on, she closed her eyes and she saw the five brothers. It was so crazy that it scared her.

Her thoughts bothered her as she stared into the mirror. That's when she thought she heard voices.

Melissa heard Charlie talking to someone outside of the dressing room door. There were multiple voices, and she wondered who was there. Closing the robe tighter against her body, she moved toward the door when suddenly there was a knock.

"Yes, who is it?" she called.

"Friends of Charlie's. He told us we could come visit you."

What the hell were they talking about? Charlie didn't mention visitors. Why would he do that?

"Sorry. I don't know anything about visitors. Go get Charlie and—"

The door opened, and one by one the five hot guys from the end of the bar came waltzing in. Melissa clutched her robe tighter and stepped back further into the room. They were way too big to fit in the small dressing room. Her breathing grew rapid and it suddenly felt tight and stuffy in the room.

"What are you guys doing back here? No one is supposed to be back here." She hated that her voice sounded so shaky and unsure, but these five men took up the small space immediately. If not for the fact that she still wore the stilettos, she would appear elflike next to them.

"Don't be frightened. We're not here to hurt you," the one guy with shoulder-length hair stated calmly. One glance at the others and they looked ready to devour her. She felt her body warm at their presence, and she wondered, what the hell was wrong? She should be deathly afraid that five extra large men crowded into her dressing room after viewing the performance she just did.

"Listen, I think you guys got the wrong impression out there. That was just an act."

"We know that. We have a proposition for you, though," one guy stated, causing his brothers to look at him as if he were crazy. Melissa picked up on it immediately.

"I'm not interested in any of your propositions," she replied as the same man moved closer. He eyed her from head to toe then licked his lips. *Damn, did he have fabulous lips. What the heck? Focus, Melissa, this could get ugly.*

"I think you got the wrong idea. I don't do sex for money," she stated firmly, but her voice cracked on the last syllable as the guy moved closer to her. Her hip pressed against the wall and then her back. Son of a bitch, he backed her into the wall.

"I'm happy to hear that you're not a whore. I expect more from my woman."

Her eyes widened in shock. Was this guy a nut job?

"Your woman?"

He reached toward her cheek, and she held his gaze as the deep, dark brown of his eyes seemed to sparkle with black flecks. Then she felt the other hand at her waist before he was inches from her body.

His thumb caressed her lower lip, and she inhaled his scent. Peculiar. He smelled familiar and interesting. Her breathing calmed, and the fear she had moments ago seemed to slowly be minimizing.

"You feel it. I know you feel it, honey. Inhale my scent and recognize the familiarity of your partner. You felt it at the bar earlier, too."

Partner? At the bar? Oh shit, he knows who I am.

She panicked and tried to push against him to get away from his hold.

* * * *

"Whoa, honey, don't freak out. Your secret's safe with us," Logan added, joining Frankie beside their mate.

"Your eyes are so beautiful. Did you really think the mask would hide them?" Logan asked as he touched her cheek. He watched her chest rise and fall, and her grip loosened on her robe. His eyes roamed over the gap in the robe, and she clenched it tighter again.

"What do you want?" she asked, eyeing him and looking concerned.

"You, Mel. We want you," Frankie whispered then pressed his lips over hers. He sensed her resistance at first, and then it appeared her body and soul recognized him as one of her mates.

He took the moment to pull her curvy body against his. He caressed her lower back as he devoured her mouth and minimized her fear. She, in return, became calm in his arms.

He didn't want to push too far and knew she needed to adjust to this situation. They knew nothing about her, and she knew nothing about them. In fact, from what he could decipher, she was human.

Slowly he released her lips and kissed her chin and neck.

"Thank you, Mel."

Her eyes looked glossy and hazed over. Could the mating musk be working so quickly?

Logan placed his fingers under her chin, tilting her head toward him.

"Do you feel the connection?" he asked her as he held her gaze.

She nodded, and his wolf celebrated inside him.

"Good. So why don't you get dressed and we'll talk about this some more?" Logan suggested.

"I can't. I have to work."

"Fuck work." Frankie began to protest, but Logan stopped Frankie and shoved Frankie behind him.

"We'll wait until your shift is over. We'll be right outside," Logan said and gave her a gentle kiss on her cheek despite the fact that his cock pounded against his jeans, demanding release. His wolf kept repeating the words "fuck and claim, fuck and claim." He felt like a fucking robot.

She stared at them, looking unsure but not quite ready to bolt, so they walked out and waited for her to come out.

* * * *

Melissa stared at herself in the mirror and touched her swollen lips. Her body was on complete fire, and her pussy wept with need. Those men were lethal, and it appeared they all wanted to have sex with her. Damn, she would have had sex with the first guy against that wall if he pushed a little harder. She shook her head at the thought. *Being sexually deprived for the last eight months has obviously made me crazy.*

She began to remove the makeup and change her clothes as she thought about what the first guy said. He asked if she felt that feeling? What was going on with her? She felt a familiarity to them, yet she never met any of the men before tonight. Maybe she should ignore them?

She thought about their sexy bodies and their amazingly good looks. Shaking her head in the mirror, she couldn't believe her own train of thought. It had been months since she had sex with one man, now little old, inexperienced her was going to take on five?

Yeah right? I think shaking your tits and ass in front of strangers has turned your brain to mush. Concentrate on studying and passing the bar, not getting laid and being used. Like being used by one guy hadn't been hell? How would being used by five be better?

Chapter 5

The five brothers watched Melissa work. She tried to avoid that end of the bar, but it was inevitable. The brothers caused a fight with Jerry in order to get her to wait on them. She had fifteen minutes until the private party. With a sigh, she raised her chin and headed into the unknown with eyes wide open.

She looked at each of them, and her insides came to life. She felt herself blush as they stared at her with eyes filled with lust and fantasies. She didn't know how she could see such things in their eyes alone, but she did. No man ever looked at her like that and definitely not five at the same time. When she looked at them, the first thoughts that came to mind were them ravishing her body. One-on-one or five-on-one, she was open to any of it.

"What can I get you?" she asked, trying hard not to really look deeply into their eyes. When she did, she felt weak and powerless. That wasn't a familiar or enticing feeling for her. Trust didn't come easy for her. She needed to be very careful. The simple fact that they were cops to boot didn't sit well with her criminal side either. *Yikes!*

"Don't you even want to know our names?" the one who kissed her so thoroughly asked. She felt herself blush again. *Get a grip, girl, or they'll think you are easy prey.*

She shrugged her shoulders nonchalantly as if she didn't care either way. One of the men raised his eyebrows in the most adorable way. She shook her head and laughed. Then they began to introduce themselves.

"I'm Logan," the first guy stated, reaching his hand out for her to shake it. She was hesitant, but his smile weakened her defenses.

"Logan, nice to meet you," she replied, shaking his hand, and the introductions continued. She smiled at the one named Vince. He seemed a bit shy compared to the others but by no means safe. He had muscles everywhere and was in great physical condition. Immediately Sunny introduced himself, taking her hand from Vince and bringing it to his lips. She held his intense gaze and felt her thighs shake when he let the tip of his tongue touch the top of her hand right before he kissed it. Her heart hammered in her chest at the thought that he wanted to see how she tasted. She should have been repulsed by the action but on the contrary her panties were drenched.

"I'm Jake," the really big guy whispered, and she wasn't sure she heard him right. Silly her leaned forward over the bar to hear him better.

"The name is Jake, baby. Damn, you smell good," he whispered as his warm, firm lips pressed against her neck and ear. The chills coated her body and quickly she pulled away. She was trying to maintain some control here, but these men were lethal. Just as she thought she had met them all, the fifth brother introduced himself. She reached out her hand to shake Frankie's hand, the guy that kissed her and his big, brown eyes held her gaze. She licked her lips out of nervousness and all the men made weird noises.

"Your lips are calling to me again, sweetheart. Why don't you lean on over and let me have another taste?" Frankie asked, and her heart instantly hammered in her chest. He was a definite tease. Handsome and experienced, and he reminded her of Colin Farrell. That bad-boy, I-can-get-into-your-pants smile of his did a number on certain body parts. She bet he probably had a mouth on him like the actor, as well. Her imagination would soar with fantasies about these men tonight, when she was alone on the couch.

"I don't think so, Frankie." She turned away as someone called her name. It was Tara, her replacement for the night. Now Melissa had to freshen up before the private party.

"Okay, guys, this is Tara. She's going to take real good care of you. It was nice meeting you all," Melissa said. The moment the words left her mouth she noticed what appeared to be shocked expressions on all five men. Logan got up from the barstool as if he could stop her. She ignored their questions as she hurried to the back exit of the bar.

As soon as she was down the hallway and about to enter the bathroom, someone grabbed her shoulder to turn her around.

She gasped as she turned to give the person a piece of her mind until she saw that it was Logan. Looking straight up at the six-feet-five-inch monster of a man, her insides quivered.

He grabbed her upper arm as a few women exited the bathroom, staring at Logan, practically drooling before they exited back to the club. She couldn't help the jealous feeling that hit her gut. Logan was an exquisite work of art. A lot of women found that appealing. Apparently, by the amount of times she felt her pussy weep with desire, she was one of them.

"What is it?" she asked him, trying to act tough.

Logan pulled her further down the hallway to where there was some privacy. He pressed her body against the wall and kept one hand pressed against the wall behind her and above her left shoulder while his other hand laid flat against the wall and next to her right hip. She was trapped between a solid wall and a massive amount of muscles. Even his forearms had rippling muscles through them. She stared up into his eyes, and he stepped one foot back to lower his frame for her, but his chest was inches from her own.

"You can't just run off like that after what we discussed in the dressing room," he reprimanded, holding her gaze with his eyes but faltering as he locked in on her lips. She licked them out of self-consciousness and saw Logan tense in response.

"You're killing me, Mel," he whispered then pressed his firm lips against her own. She found herself kissing him back and loving the feeling of his arms around her, holding her to him. His knee and leg pressed between her thighs, causing them to part as he rocked his hips against her body. She felt his hard cock hit her belly, and she gasped as he kissed her. He tasted sweet and warm as she fought him for control of the kiss. Her nipples hardened and her pussy dripped with desire as she heard Logan growl in her mouth.

Oh man, Logan's kiss was as lethal as Frankie's. If they all kissed like this she was in some serious trouble. *What the hell am I thinking? Multiple partner relationships don't really happen. They're fuck-fests and orgies where one woman comes out as a total used slut.*

Melissa pressed her palms against his chest, and Logan seemed to get the message.

"Get a room, Logan!" some guy stated, interrupting them, and Melissa turned her head away shyly and into Logan's chest.

She heard his rapid breathing and was relieved that she wasn't the only one affected by the kiss.

His hand gently caressed her cheek as he continued to hold her to him.

The sound of his raspy voice caused tiny vibrations to travel up her legs. Suddenly, she wished there was a bed nearby.

"Sorry about that. I didn't expect to get so carried away," he said and continued to caress her skin then rub his thumb against her lower lip. Call her crazy, but he sounded sincere.

"I want your number. Can I have it so we can call you?"

She looked around and saw that Spike was standing nearby watching her. He mouthed the words, "Are you okay?" and she smiled and nodded. Spike still gave Logan a dirty look in challenge, and Logan gave a light snort. He was way bigger than Spike, and something told her he had secret weapons of his own. She heard the men talking about the SWAT team, and some guys referred to Logan as commander.

Logan looked back at Melissa and pulled out his cell phone.

"What's your number, baby?" he asked, and the sound of his voice and the way he called her "baby" sent chills through her. Man, she must be desperate for sex.

"I don't give my number out to strangers," she replied.

His hand pressed against her ribs, and his thumb slightly grazed the under part of her breast. He gave her a quick kiss on her lips then licked his own lips as if she tasted like a dessert. Her nipples instantly hardened, and her mind yelled for her to give the man her damn number.

"We're not strangers, Mel. Not after that kiss we just shared. Come on. I promise that my brothers and I will be gentlemen," he began to beg like a pro. He gently rubbed his thumb over her bottom lip and inhaled against her neck. She contemplated, and her silence made him try harder.

"Mel! Charlie said five minutes!" Spike yelled down the hallway. Melissa tried to move, but Logan stopped her by blocking her path.

"I have to go, and I still need to use the ladies' room and freshen up."

"I'll just wait until you come out, and I won't let you get to the party until—"

"785…" She began to give him her cell number.

"Do you have your cell on you?" he asked, and she nodded. Then he dialed the number on his cell, and he saw that her cell phone began to ring.

"Didn't trust me, huh?" she asked, crossing her arms in front of her chest.

"No, but you'll make up for it later," he teased then kissed her cheek before she walked into the ladies' room.

* * * *

"So we're just going to fucking leave her here?" Vince asked.

"Listen, guys, she's not were. She doesn't know how this works. Right now, we're probably coming off as some overaggressive men looking for sex. We need to pace ourselves and gain her trust," Logan said as he began leading everyone out of the club. As they exited the building, they saw a small convoy of limos and black SUVs in front of the entrance.

"That must be the people for the private party," Jake stated then stopped walking.

"What are you doing?" Vince asked.

"I'm checking out the guests. Our fucking mate is going to be in there, and we can't gain access to the private party."

"I got Mel's cell number. Let's leave it at that for now. The bartender said that Mel is working tomorrow night. We'll come back," Logan added, and they continued down the street and around the corner to their own SUV.

* * * *

"Okay, Mel, do you have everything that was on the list?" Charlie asked, sounding very nervous. More so than usual.

"Yes, what the hell is the big deal?" she asked, and he closed his eyes then exhaled. "I'm sorry. I'm just tense. Bret is bringing some important people here, and if all goes well, this can be great for business. I can make a shitload of money, and so can you."

"Bret?" she asked, and just then the piece of shit entered the room with his two goons Felix and Deatrix.

He smirked at her as if he had the upper hand. The asshole would have to do more than request her as his bartender for some private party before she would jump into bed with him ever again.

She rolled her eyes and continued to prep the bar.

Charlie greeted Bret with the utmost respect and ass-kissing she had ever seen. She lost some respect for her friend right then and there. Bret was nothing but a leech. He took whatever he wanted and needed from people then tossed them away like dirt. He had wanted her to be his main fuck, and thankfully for her, she didn't accept his verbal contract. It would have been upheld to the fullest, and she would probably be dead or so juiced up on meth she wouldn't know who she was spreading her legs for. Her blood felt as if it were boiling with hostility. If she could she would walk out right now, but one look at Charlie's pleading face and she knew she was stuck. She might as well make the best of it.

As she prepared Bret's dirty martini, adding a little dirty water to the fucker's cocktail, she saw the rest of the crew arrive. Deatrix and Felix did their thing, frisking down the guests and checking for guns or other weapons. This was going to be a long fucking night.

As she listened to some of the bimbos talk and made them their Malibu Bay Breezes and Sex on the Beaches she observed the two men she recognized as Carlos and Chico along with their three guards. She swallowed hard, remembering that they weren't the most upstanding citizens in the room. They could surely give Bret a run for his money. Never mind the fact that she was the one who recently ripped them off. She swallowed hard and released an uneasy breath.

Melissa served some light hors d'oeuvres along with Chu, a servant of Bret's that went with him on most excursions involving food.

"Would you like some shrimp, sir?" she asked Carlos, and he eyed her from head to toe but mostly stared at her cleavage.

He smirked then winked as he took a shrimp, dipped it in the cocktail sauce, and stared at her as if she would be turned on.

"It's so nice to see you, Melissa," he stated then placed his hand against her thigh. She would have loved to pull away, but that wouldn't be smart. The man could kill with looks alone.

She smiled appreciatively as if pleased that he remembered her.

"Nice to see you, too, sir."

He chuckled, and she stood up straight to move toward Chico so he could have a shrimp.

He blatantly eyed her ass and reached to touch it, but she casually moved toward Bret to offer him the tray of food.

"What's this 'sir' stuff, Melissa?" Carlos asked as he leaned back in the chair and took in the full sight of her. She knew his game, and she could play him as well as he thought he was playing her.

"I've often fantasized about your voice saying my name," he teased then took a sip from his vodka and tonic.

"Ahh...I have shared the same dream, my friend, except in mine she is moaning *my* name," Chico added, and they chuckled.

"I've got you both beat because mine was not a fantasy but a reality," Bret stated proudly as he caressed her ass and pulled her closer.

Melissa pulled away as the other men roared.

"Lucky fucking bastard. I didn't know she was yours," Carlos said then took another shrimp from the platter that Melissa set down on the table.

"That's because I'm not his, Carlos," she stated then looked at Bret. "Plus, one not-so-satisfying fuck could hardly bind me to any man."

Carlos and Chico roared with laughter as they nearly spilled their drinks. One look at Bret and she saw that he was irritated, and his eyes looked very strange.

He stood up and grabbed her by the arm.

Squeezing her upper arm tightly, he whispered in her ear, but his words cut short as he inhaled next to her. What was up with men sniffing her lately? Did her deodorant stop working? She wanted to sniff her own pits, but she didn't want to make it obvious.

"We'll talk later. Show some respect, or I'll offer you to them for dessert." He squeezed her arm hard enough to cause bruising then abruptly released it.

Chu gave her a warning look, indicating that he saw it was a close call as well. She knew she shouldn't have gotten so upset so quickly, but Bret put her on edge.

* * * *

The time passed slowly with the three assholes talking about drug deals, money, and then something interesting that caught her attention. She thought she heard incorrectly, but then Bret tossed the words around. "African diamonds."

Her ears perked up, but she hid her interest from the men. Chu came over and began talking with her. She was good at conversing with one person while listening in on other conversations, and it had served her well in the past.

"So, how is your aunt?" Chu asked.

Melissa smiled. Chu was a nice guy despite his professional position, if she could call it professional.

"She just came home the other day. She looks good, and the doctors think they got all the cancer."

"That's fantastic news," he stated, leaning closer and covering her hand with his own. He paused close to her, and when she looked up, his eyes held a look of concern. He and Melissa picked at the cherries from the container at the bar.

"What?" she asked him, and he glanced toward Bret then back at her.

"Who have you been hanging out with lately?"

She had the feeling something was up with Chu's line of questioning.

"No one, why?"

"No new guy in your life?"

She chuckled. "Yeah, like I want to go down that road again."

He laughed halfheartedly.

"Did you meet a guy tonight, at the bar?"

Her eyes widened, and she glanced at Bret. He looked at Carlos, but she had a feeling he could hear Chu's question.

"Just some guys, why?"

"Did you fuck them?" he asked with a shaky voice.

"Chu! What the hell kind of question is that?"

He shrugged his shoulders, trying to pull off nonchalant, but he failed miserably. Her defenses were immediately up.

"Why do you care?"

"I assumed that you're particular about who you are intimate with. I can smell men's cologne on you."

The word *oh* covered her lips in response.

She felt bad for being uptight and snapping at him. She blushed for getting busted making out with two complete strangers, but Chu didn't have to know the details.

"I'm sorry. I'm just tired. It's really no big deal. I met a few different guys tonight."

"Well, be careful, Mel. Sometimes things aren't always as they appear."

"You don't have to say that twice."

He covered her hand again, and he held her gaze.

"Be careful who you kiss. Sometimes men can be such animals."

She got the chills from his statement and couldn't understand why she had the feeling he meant something more to that statement. Instead of pursuing the topic, he began to talk about the club.

"It is so crowded in there tonight. I heard that some new stripper Lola made a surprise visit and knocked their socks off."

She tried to hide her blush as she chuckled and nearly choked on the cherry she just popped into her mouth. If he only knew that it had been her, pretending to be Lola for Lilly. She had heard the gossip spread at the bar that Lola only did special events and that she was in the witness protection program. She chuckled to herself. Poor Lilly. Melissa figured she had better make a point in calling Lilly and explaining what happened. Who would have known the Lola performance Melissa did would create such gossip.

"Yeah, she did a real hot number. The bachelor party was rocking. I think the party is still going strong now," she added.

Chu moved closer and whispered. "To think, right outside that door about a hundred cops are hanging out, and inside here major criminal scams are being discussed. It's fucking crazy sometimes."

The mention of the word cops made her think of Logan, Frankie, Vince, Sunny, and Jake. They really were exceptional-looking men. She wanted to know more about them, but she was scared. A relationship would never work. Sure, she was attracted to them, but she wanted more than just sexual flings. She wanted a normal life with normal things.

"Hey, what's the long face for?"

"Nothing. Just thinking if I'll ever be able to live a normal life."

"What's not normal about this?" he asked, gesturing to encompass the room.

She looked at the Asian man's soft smile. He was handsome with dark black hair and light green eyes. The ladies often flirted with him, but he appeared to be flamboyant. She never asked him about dating, and truth be told, she really didn't want to know. It wasn't like Chu and she were friends. They were just stuck working for bosses that had a final say in tonight's gig.

"Chu, get real, will ya. Don't you think about getting old and settling down somewhere with a house, kids, and a normal life?"

"You're fucking twenty-two years old, Melissa. You shouldn't be worried about getting old. You should be planning your next love-fest or sex partner and living it up."

She chuckled at his carefree description.

"I've got kids to take care of and bills to pay."

His smile disappeared, and he covered her hand again, giving her a sympathetic smile.

* * * *

"Chu, bring the ladies outside for us. Get them some drinks," Bret stated, calling to Chu.

"Melissa, can I get another drink?" Chico asked as he leaned against the bar. He watched her make the martini, and she wondered if he thought she would poison him. He wasn't worth going to jail for. Bret was a different story.

Speak of the shithead, he walked behind her and placed his hands on her hips.

"She makes a mean martini, doesn't she, Chico?" Bret asked as Chico sipped from the glass. He never took his eyes off of her.

Again, Bret sniffed her neck and pressed his body against her back.

"Who have you been hanging out with tonight, Mel?" he asked, and she knew that tone. He wanted names, and he wouldn't ask twice.

"No one in particular."

His arm came around her waist, and he pulled her off balance to the side. She had to hold on to his arm or she would fall.

He raised his eyebrows.

She wondered if he could smell men's cologne on her. Were the brothers wearing cologne?

"Dating anyone, Melissa?" Chico asked.

She shook her head.

"The place is filled with cops tonight. She brushed up against some—"

"We have business to discuss. Mel's my business, not yours. Let's get this over with, so I can be done with you," Bret stated, and Melissa wondered what the hell was happening. Bret cut Chico off, and now he acted like he hated the man.

Carlos joined them, and they began to talk about some drugs being delivered to a safe house in Queens and about some deliveries to parties this weekend. One house in New Jersey had its own cocaine and methamphetamine manufacturing lab in the basement.

They talked about a couple of guys who could deliver some drugs to a guy named Vito on the east side of Brooklyn and about money for some hit needing to be picked up tomorrow night. When they said one hundred and fifty grand, her heart nearly pounded from her chest.

They were so confident that they didn't need a bunch of trained people on these deliveries. They figured they weren't being watched and that no one would suspect anything. Especially if they sent in some skull heads to do the job. When Carlos mentioned Lester Crowe, she nearly laughed out loud. That crackhead didn't know his left from his right. But she had to remind herself that she wasn't going to do another hit. She had plenty of money. Her aunt and the kids were fine, and she could slowly wean herself out of this life and into a better, more legit lifestyle.

* * * *

By three o'clock in the morning, Chu, Carlos, and Chico were leaving, giving her kisses good-bye. Carlos slipped a tight roll of hundred-dollar bills the size of a thick cigarette into her cleavage. He gave one breast a little squeeze then nibbled her neck. When she looked at him as Chico gently nudged him forward, she noticed his eyes looked as if they were glowing. She blinked a couple of times, and Chu said something drawing their attention toward him.

Chico slid an arm around her waist and whispered in her ear.

"Be careful, sweetheart, and watch out for wolves." He gave her ass a tap then pulled her hand to his lips and kissed the top of it. Then he placed a brass bill clip filled with bills into her hand. The top bill was a fifty, but she was certain the others were larger.

She swallowed hard, said thank you, and began to clean up the bar. As she walked around the room cleaning up their mess, she placed the glasses in the sink to clean behind the bar then went back around the room, fluffing pillows and dusting off the tables.

She heard someone come back in, but she thought it was Charlie.

"I'm almost finished. What a long night," she stated then felt an arm go around her waist and Bret's chin on her shoulder. He was an inch shy of six feet tall, but he towered over her five-foot-five-inch frame. She tensed immediately and prayed he wasn't drunk.

"Let go of me, Bret. The party's over."

She attempted to wiggle out of his embrace.

"I think the party's just begun, Mel. And besides, I won the bet."

"What bet? What the hell are you talking about?" she demanded to know as she twisted out of his embrace.

"One of us was going to take you home tonight and fuck you. I won."

"You're out of your mind, Bret. Just get your shit and go."

She attempted to walk past him, but he grabbed her wrist and pulled her back against him. The pain radiated up her arm, causing her to lower nearly to her knees.

"I didn't know you were into wolves, Mel. We're gonna have a fucking incredible time tonight."

"Wolves? What the hell are you saying? I think you're drunk."

He twisted harder, and she felt the skin pinch. She would surely have a bruise.

"Don't play games with me. I can smell the Valdamar wolves all over your neck. Their saliva is on your skin."

"Who are the Valdamar wolves, and what in god's name do you mean that their saliva is on my neck—"

The smack came out of nowhere, knocking against her jaw and neck. She fell to the floor, holding her face where he hit her.

Frantically, she scooted on her hands backwards as he moved closer. That's when she saw his eyes glowing. He was some kind of freak.

"Get away from me!" she screamed in fear for her life. What was he?

"You take me for a fool, Mel. You know that my kind exists, and you sit here flaunting an enemy's scent in my face? In front of clients of mine? I should rip your fucking jugular out."

He reached down and pulled her up and against him. He kissed her brutally hard, shoving his tongue into her mouth, causing her to gag. She pounded her fists against his chest, not even hearing the door swing open and both Charlie and Spike coming to her rescue.

They pulled Bret off of her, and Spike pulled him up. Bret's eyes glowed, and his teeth looked larger, as if he were some kind of animal. Melissa held on to Charlie.

"Calm the fuck down, Bret. Get out of here now!" Charlie yelled.

"I'm not done with her," Bret stated as Spike took him out of the room.

Charlie tried to calm her down.

"Oh my god, Charlie, he's not human. He's crazy, and his eyes…his eyes." Charlie pulled her into his arms and held her against his chest.

"It's going to be okay, Mel."

"How can you be so calm? He nearly killed me."

"We got to you in time. Just try to stay clear of him, Mel."

"You don't have to tell me twice. Besides, you're the one who booked me for this party," she stated sarcastically. Her heart rate was beginning to calm as Charlie released his hold on her.

"There are people out there who have the ability to change, Mel. There are some good, and there are some bad."

"Change? What do you mean change their eyes when they're angry?"

"Wolves. Now it's too much to get into right now. You're safe, and Bret's out of here."

Melissa looked around the room. "What about this mess? What if he comes after me again?"

"I'll take care of it. Why don't you head home, and we'll talk about this tomorrow."

Chapter 6

"What the fuck kind of party goes on until three o'clock in the fucking morning?" Jake asked as they stared at the clock in the SUV that they parked next to Melissa's car.

By four o'clock they were ready to storm the place when suddenly Melissa emerged with both Spike and Charlie walking her to her car.

Immediately upon seeing them exit the SUV, Melissa cuddled closer to Charlie.

Jake had a bad feeling in the pit of his stomach.

"What's going on?"

"Yeah, what happened?" Frankie asked, moving next to Melissa, filled with just as much concern as his brothers.

"We had a little situation. It's under control," Charlie stated.

"What the fuck kind of situation? She looks scared out of her mind," Logan asked as he looked Melissa over, noticing her ripped shirt. Immediately his eyes glowed, and Melissa cried out, "You, too!" and then turned against Charlie's chest.

Charlie explained what had gone down.

"That piece of shit is a dead man," Sunny added.

"I just want to go home. Please just leave me alone and let me go home," Melissa cried.

"Give me her keys," Logan demanded, and Charlie handed them over.

"I'll drive her," he told Charlie then began to help her to the car.

She stood still and stared at him as if he could hurt her.

"I swear I won't hurt you. My brothers and I would never cause you harm."

She looked to Charlie for reassurance, and he pulled her into another embrace.

"You will be safest with the Valdamar brothers."

"Valdamar?"

Sunny walked her to the passenger side and helped her get into the car. Then he walked over to the SUV along with his brothers and prepared to follow them home.

* * * *

"Why would Bret go after her?" Frankie asked as they followed Logan.

"He smelled us on her and assumed we were intimate," Vince suggested.

"Could be, or he has a thing for her and knew we were interested as well," Jake added.

"We can't let him near her. He's such a fucking slimeball," Frankie replied.

"Charlie may be right and Bret was just jealous. He said that Bret and Melissa went out a couple of times," Jake stated.

"I don't even want to think that he fucked her," Frankie replied.

"She's ours now, so it doesn't matter who she was with. We have to make her understand about our culture and why we're here to help the humans," Sunny added very seriously.

"Maybe Logan will make some progress with her during the car ride," Jake stated.

* * * *

Melissa felt as if she was having some sort of weird out-of-body experience. She had seen strange things. Perhaps this was some crazy nightmare she would wake up from soon. Then she thought about the entire night. The Valdamar brothers showed up out of nowhere and made her feel horny and ready to jump into an orgy with them. She stripped on stage to help out Lilly, and now she's some celebrity with the men at the club. Then Bret reserves the private room and requests her for this whole meeting with Carlos and Chico, and it turns out he's a wolf as well as a man. Their eyes had changed color when they spoke to her and when Carlos handed her the money. Come to think of it, so did Chu's, and he was the one warning her about men being animals and things not being as they may appear. Did she just enter the Twilight Zone?

As the information processed in her head, she looked at Logan. The man was the perfect specimen of male, and he also looked aggressive. Not like he could shift into some kind of four-legged beast, but intimidating in a way she wasn't used to seeing.

"What are you?" she whispered as she turned her body toward him and pressed her back against the door.

"I'm not going to lie to you, Melissa."

She snorted in disbelief, and he actually gave her an annoyed expression. Her gut told her this guy was important and no one ever questioned him. Tough shit! She was asking every fucking question she wanted, and he was going to give her a straight answer.

"We're shifters."

"And that means what?"

"It means that we can shift into wolves whenever we need to."

"How does it work?"

"It's something we were born into. A family gene passed down from generation to generation. Wolf packs are not uncommon. It's just that we all keep our abilities hidden from humans."

"Because we'd want to destroy you?" she asked, even though it was meant as a statement.

"You couldn't if you tried," he replied confidently, and again she got the chills from the fierceness and truth of his tone.

She couldn't help but think about Bret and the way his eyes changed and how he grabbed her. She must have flinched when she closed her eyes because suddenly she felt Logan's hand take her hand and gently pull her closer to him.

She was scared, but her instincts told her she didn't have to be with Logan.

"Did he hurt you?" he asked. His voice sounded weird.

She nodded but kept her distance as she looked at her wrist.

Logan released her hand and softly lifted her jacket sleeve up to see her other wrist.

"Does it hurt?"

"I'll be fine," she whispered, but the tears rolled down her cheek, and she couldn't wipe them away fast enough.

Thank God they arrived at her apartment complex.

He parked the car, and they both got out. The others pulled up and joined her and Logan.

He reached for her hand to examine her wrist in the light from the lamp post.

"I'll be fine," she whispered, her voice cracking as she realized just how big of a man Logan was. Her small hand was lost in his much larger hand. His fingers lightly grazed the delicate flesh on her wrists and she felt the bruising. She attempted to pull away, but the others were near now, too, and she found herself moving closer to Logan.

Looking up into his dark brown eyes, he held her gaze as he brought her wrist to his lips and kissed her skin.

She closed her eyes, feeling that deep connection again and then his arm going around her waist, pulling her against his chest.

"Is she okay? Did he hurt her?" Sunny asked, sounding upset, and his voice frightened her. Instantly she pulled from Logan's arms.

She held out her hand palm up. "My keys?"

Logan crossed his arms in front of his chest and leaned against the hood of her car as if he had control because he held her keys. The group of them surrounded her in a semicircle in front of her car.

"Keep them. I don't care right now." She attempted to leave but walked into Frankie. He pulled her against his chest and hugged her. She struggled just for a second then allowed him to hold her.

* * * *

"I can smell his scent on her," Frankie stated to his brothers.

"Just deal with it like I did for the fifteen minute ride over here," Logan replied.

"I need to go. I'm exhausted and need some ice and some painkillers," Melissa stated as she pulled away from Frankie. He held his arms around her waist and looked her in the eyes.

"We're going to have to talk. It would be better if we come inside—"

"No! No, you can't come inside. You need to leave. You can't come in with me," she stated then pulled away and clutched her jacket to her chest.

"What's wrong? Why not?" Frankie asked.

"Because I have kids and my aunt lives there, too. My friend and her kids are there as well. I need to go. I really don't want any trouble. I promise that I won't say a word about tonight. Good-bye." She swiftly began to run up the sidewalk.

"Wait, the keys, Melissa," Logan stated, and she turned toward them.

"Throw them to me," she said, and Logan hesitated then tossed her the keys. She caught them and hurriedly entered the front door to the building.

* * * *

"She has fucking kids?" Vince asked, sounding shocked.

They were all silent.

"We have some work to do before we go see her tomorrow night at Charlie's," Logan said, and they all got into the SUVs.

"What about that piece of shit, Bret? We should pay the fucker a visit," Vince said, shocking his brothers. He was the calm one out of all of them. He and Jake were levelheaded, and it took a lot to piss them off. Sunny and Frankie had the short fuses while Logan tried to maintain control and the peace.

"No. We need to focus on Melissa first. We have to find out her story and everything about her life and these kids she has. Was she married? Is the guy alive or dead?"

"Fuck, Logan. I'm feeling so out of sorts right now. How the hell can you be so organized?" Vince asked.

"I have to be. This situation could become out of control very quickly if not handled accordingly."

Chapter 7

Melissa tiptoed her way into the apartment and found all the kids sleeping on sleeping bags and blankets in the living room. It was a good old-fashioned slumber party. Celine was on the couch watching over them, and Melissa smiled. They were all so innocent. They had no idea what kind of a messed-up, crazy world was out there. Now it appeared that men who could shift into wolves walked the earth as well. She got the chills, and then she thought of the brothers again. A SWAT team for the NYPD no less, and probably the most lethal force a human could reckon with.

She walked into the kitchen, grabbed a bottle of water, and absorbed the silence in the room and the sound of peaceful breathing.

Then came thoughts of Bret and the way his eyes changed and how he practically attacked her. She was so scared. Almost as scared as when those bullets whizzed past her the other night when she robbed the drug dealers.

With a sigh, she walked around the counter then heard Celine's voice.

"Everything okay?" she whispered as she slowly raised her head up from the couch.

Melissa clutched her jacket tighter against her chest, feeling her wrist throb but hoping that Celine couldn't see her ripped shirt.

"Yeah, fine. Sorry if I woke you."

"No. I'm a light sleeper. It's a curse from years in the shelter."

"How did tonight go?"

"Great. The kids had a ball and insisted on having a slumber party. They want to do it again tomorrow." Celine glanced at the clock on the DVD player by the TV. "Well, I mean tonight. You're working at Paul's, right?" Celine asked, and Melissa felt her heart pound in her chest. The guys wanted to see her tomorrow. Tonight had been a nightmare. Maybe a change of scene was in order.

"Yeah. I spoke to him this morning. I'd better head to bed. I'm sure the kids will be up early and want French toast for breakfast."

"Chocolate chip pancakes," Brandon whispered from his pillow, and they laughed.

"Go back to sleep," Melissa whispered then smiled at Celine before heading into the bathroom.

* * * *

Melissa peeled the clothes from her body and placed them in a garbage bag. She needed to get rid of these before anyone saw them and questioned her. A glance in the mirror and she saw the scratch by her neck but no bruising so far on her cheek. Bret had hit her pretty hard, and she hoped there wouldn't be bruising there by morning.

Her wrist looked slightly black and blue but the bruise was not really noticeable. She would wear a bunch of tiny beaded bracelets to Paul's and no one would even notice.

She turned on the faucet in the shower and started the hot water. Stepping under the gentle spray, she smelled the mixed scents of Bret's cologne and Logan's scent, as well as Frankie's. *Great. Now they have me sniffing things.*

She quickly grabbed the bottle of body wash, letting the aroma fill her nostrils and the bad memories disappear. As she covered the washcloth with body wash, she cleansed her body, spending extra time caressing her breasts as thoughts of Logan filled her mind.

She remembered the way he confined her between his arms and how his fingers brushed against the underside of her breast. Then she thought about the way he kissed her. It was hot and ended way too soon. She had forgotten that they were in the hallway in the club. Her belly tingled with a mix of embarrassment and stimulation, and soon she thought about how Logan and Frankie kissed her. She thought about Frankie. Melissa knew what kind of a man he was. He could get action any time he wanted it. He had a temper, and he was demanding. The way he cornered her so quickly like a prey corners its next meal burned her insides as the moisture funneled down her core. She dropped the washcloth and slowly pressed her fingers to her thighs, gently caressing the *V* between her legs, and straight to her pussy lips. They were wet, all right, and not from the water as she pressed a dainty digit to her cunt. Her cream coated her fingers, and curiosity made her press them back to her folds.

Closing her eyes, she played with her labia and rotated her finger, letting the cream coat her lips as she rubbed the sensitive flesh.

In her mind, she envisioned Jake, including his attire and his crew-cut hair. Dressed in designer jeans and a button-down shirt, she knew his type. Classy and sophisticated. She pressed her finger into her hole. What would it be like to make love to him? To all of them?

Melissa envisioned each of the brothers surrounding her on a large bed, their thick, muscular bodies surrounding her own. Long, thick, solid cocks fisted and ready to love every inch of her, one hole at a time.

She added a second finger and increased her speed, feeling her knuckles tighten as she tried to pump faster. Her insides coiled up, but she just couldn't reach her peak. She added another digit, attempting to locate that special spot no man had ever found on her. She finger-fucked herself in the shower thinking about her men. Her men? Was she really considering having sex with them? How could it work? Her hazy mind fought a seemingly worthless battle against her desires. She imagined herself laid out over Logan, riding him as best she could as Jake fucked her in the ass. Her mouth opened as the warm water cascaded over her lips and on her tongue. She imagined Frankie's cock in her mouth. He would love that. He would probably hold her hair in a controlling manner as he fucked her mouth. The idea of having sex with more than one man at once was never even a fantasy. She never let anyone touch her anus, yet here she was so willingly imagining the brothers exploring every orifice of her body. She moaned at the vision in her mind, feeling her body tighten as if it were really happening. Her mouth opened wider as the water splashed inside and against her sensitive nipples. She continued to pump into her own pussy, hearing the water slosh against her fingers, the cream, and her flesh. She had a fabulous imagination and the men had left quite an impression on her body. Just the thought of them, even with her eyes closed, made her fantasy feel so real. She actually felt Frankie come down her throat as she swallowed his warm essence and gulped for air. He pulled out, and then Sunny caressed her chin and pressed his long, thick cock between her wet, parted lips, and she sucked him in, unable to handle his girth. Jake pulled her left nipple and fondled her breast as Vince pulled her right, and she lost it. She gritted her teeth as an explosive orgasm overtook her body. Gasping for air, she tried to quiet her panting and hoped that no one had heard her.

* * * *

"What have we got so far on our little stripper?" Frankie asked as he bit into a juicy, red apple.

Sunny growled, obviously still upset about their mate's line of work. Frankie didn't mind so much now that they found her. She would only be doing the striptease for him and his brothers from here on out.

"Don't joke around. I'm still trying to swallow the whole thing,"

Sunny stated as he pulled up a picture of some woman who looked just like Melissa.

"I don't mind one bit. It will make bedroom play more interesting, especially when we install our own pole. Any ideas where the best spot will be?"

"You're fucking serious, aren't you?"

"Hell yeah, Sunny! Did you see her moves?"

"Just shut the fuck up, all right. I'm trying to gather everything I can on her. Logan's going be back any minute."

Just then the door opened and both Logan and Jake arrived.

"Hey, what's going on? Where's Vince?" Frankie asked, taking another bite of apple.

"Doing recon on our girl. How did you make out, Sunny?" Logan asked, walking closer to the computer.

"Okay, this is what I have so far. Here's a picture of her sister and her sister's husband. They died in a drive-by shooting two years ago. Apparently he was a detective in narcotics, but I don't remember him," Sunny said.

"Well, the date stated May nineteenth. We were in Colombia all of May, then doing that job in Singapore in April. We missed the whole thing," Jake stated as he leaned his butt against the desk.

"Well, Melissa 'Mel' Savianno is twenty-two years old, looks like she has been pursuing a law degree, and either hasn't qualified for the bar exam yet or hasn't passed. She is the legal guardian for Lea, age twelve, Brandon, age eight, and Tommy, age three, the children of Michael and Sarah Mercer."

"Not her own kids. Their her dead sister's kids?" Frankie asked.

Sunny nodded.

"What else?" Jake asked.

"We got her address, which we already know, her place of employment, and there are a few articles here about some volunteer work she's done for the local soup kitchen in her neighborhood."

"What are you not sharing with us?" Logan pushed.

Sunny exhaled as he pulled up an old police report.

"She has a criminal record?" Frankie inquired, moving closer to the screen.

"She was picked up last year for trespassing and possession of stolen property. Charlie bailed her out."

Logan released a sigh then leaned back against the couch just a few feet away from the computer and desk.

"Looks like we're going to have our hands full here. I don't get the feeling that our little vixen is going to come to us willingly. We need to make a plan here. Something that can get us some alone time with her and set things straight. I also think she's not so fragile. Don't let her petite appearance fool you. She's got secrets, and she's got weapons of her own. Dig back to her childhood, if you can, Sunny. I want to know what kind of life this kid had."

"I'm already all over it, brother. Check this out."

Sunny clicked a button on the FBI website and entered his secure password. Immediately information about Melissa filled the screen. They had her parents' names, her high school and college transcripts, and soon a little bit of an idea about how Melissa grew up. Thirty minutes later, Vince was calling from his cell phone.

* * * *

"What's up?" Logan asked as he set the phone on speaker so his brothers could hear.

"Melissa, her kids, some lady with three other kids, and an old lady in a wheelchair are sitting in the park behind the apartment building."

"The older lady is Melissa's aunt. She just had massive surgery to remove stage three cancer. She's supposedly in remission. Damn! It looks like it was a pretty expensive and intense surgery. The bill was over ninety thousand dollars," Sunny told them.

"Whoowee. That's a lot of money," Frankie stated.

"I don't think stripping and bartending pays that well, do you, Logan?" Jake asked.

Logan was not looking happy from Frankie's perspective.

"I'm getting a bad feeling," Vince said.

"So are we. I'm wondering just how long she was involved with Bret," Jake offered.

"We can find out from Charlie," Vince suggested.

"Yeah, well, we'll see him tonight when we check on Melissa. Why don't you give her some time with her family, then I'll text her about getting together tonight," Logan suggested, and Vince agreed then hung up the phone.

"You want to leave her unattended?" Frankie asked.

"She's not a perpetrator from a case, Frankie, she's our mate," Logan replied as he began to pull out his phone.

"Well, then I guess all we can do is wait for tonight," Sunny said as he looked at the screen, wondering what other secrets their little dancer had.

Chapter 8

"So, the outfit's not really that bad, right?" Paul asked as he watched Melissa stock the private bar.

She chuckled.

"Is that a 'yes, sir' or a 'whatever you say, asshole' kind of reply?" he teased.

She looked at him straight-faced and said, "You're not an asshole."

He laughed as he continued to watch her.

"What's so funny?" they heard someone ask, and a group of guys entered the private room.

"Hey, Mel, what are you doing here?" Jamie asked as he quickly made his way to her by the bar.

Paul watched as Melissa allowed Jamie to hug her then twirl her around before setting her down to look at her.

"Damn, woman, you've grown up. How the hell did you let Paul talk you into wearing this shirt?" Jamie asked then gave Paul a disapproving look but still remained holding Melissa around the waist.

"It's good to see you, Jamie. It's been a while," Melissa said then eased her way out of his arms.

Paul thought Jamie looked like he had reunited with a lost love. He cleared his throat, and the other guys introduced themselves to Melissa. She had them chugging beers and talking football in less than two minutes.

"We're expecting a few more guys from our narcotics division. They should be here any minute. We're going to meet for about an hour then eat some dinner and have some drinks. It shouldn't be that late of a night," Paul stated as he stood next to her behind the bar.

She smiled at him. "No problem. Whatever you need, just let me know. I can wait in the other room while you meet, and you can send Jamie out to get me when you're ready."

She poured another beer for one of the cops as her cell phone beeped.

"Oh, I'm sorry. I forgot to turn it off," Melissa apologized.

"No problem, honey," Paul stated.

"Boyfriend?" Jamie inquired with a smile.

Melissa's cheeks turned red.

"No. Not really."

"Good. Just maybe, my luck is changing," Jamie replied with a smile.

* * * *

Melissa politely smiled back at Jamie. He had always been a flirt, but also a nice guy and a good friend to her brother-in-law Mike. Jamie was at least five years older than her, had been engaged at one point, and then called it off for some unknown reason. He was nice-looking, with thick, blond hair and hazel eyes. Not such a bad body either, just a little thick around the waist, but in no way would she consider him fat. He was husky and muscular. He kind of reminded her of Russell Crowe. But if she was at all honest with herself, she would admit that she wasn't interested in him, but instead the five separate texts she received from the SWAT team brothers.

"Okay, guys, let's get started," Paul stated as the men all gathered around the large table.

Melissa began to walk away from the bar when some guy, a lieutenant, called her name.

"Melissa. You stay. We'll need you in a few minutes." Then he began his meeting.

Why did he want her to stay? What did he mean by needing her in a few minutes?

Damn it, if Paul turned out to be a pervert and the rest of the bunch as well and they expected her to perform or something else, he was a dead man.

Paul must have noticed her panicked expression.

"Melissa, don't look so scared. We're not going to attack you. We're all cops here. We knew your brother-in-law, Mike, and sister, Sarah, well. Just sit back and relax," he stated, and then their conversation began.

Melissa felt that twinge of uneasiness at the mention of Sarah and Mike. She also had a pinch of guilt for all her criminal behavior in the past few years. She made her bed. She had to sleep in it. Just then, her phone vibrated against her hip. When she looked down, she saw it was Logan again. Swallowing hard, she realized that thoughts of beds, criminal activity, and gaining the interest of so many cops in the last twenty-four hours spelled trouble. Her hands were tied. There was no way she could sneak out of here. She would just have to wait and see.

She took a seat on the stool and began to read the texts while she also listened in on the conversation taking place just ten feet from the bar.

Where are you? You promised to meet us today! Vince.

You're not at Charlie's, so where are you? We need to talk. Sunny.

I thought about you all night. I need those sexy lips of yours again. Don't be a naughty girl. I'd hate to punish you. Frankie.

She swallowed hard at all their texts and especially at Frankie's threat of punishment. She should have been frightened, but instead, her temperature rose and her pussy wept with need for them. How could they affect her in such a way? She didn't know any of them. They're not even human. She doesn't even know what it all means.

Feeling confused, she looked down at the last couple of texts. It was obvious that Logan gave his brothers her number. He liked to share. That was putting it mildly. They all wanted to share her. Her breath caught in her throat, and she had to clear it in order to pull herself together.

It would be in your best interest to contact one of us. Jake.

Yikes! It appeared Jake could be just as fierce as Logan.

When we find you, we won't let you go. Logan.

As the men in the room discussed some sort of investigative operation, she heard the word *Charlie* and paid more attention to the meeting than to the texts. She would have to face those men tomorrow.

* * * *

"So the investigation is at an immediate standstill. We don't know where the main distribution center is, where the new location of the secret meetings will be taking place, all because we lost our inside man," Lieutenant Sparks stated.

"I can't believe they took him out like that. How the hell was his cover blown?" Jamie asked.

"These guys are good, and with the recent surprise robberies amongst the smaller delivery guys, the higher-ups are on edge," Detective Simon Burrow added.

"Yeah, what do we have on those robberies? Any suspects?" Jamie asked.

"No, nothing concrete, anyway. Although, there may be a possibility that my original theory is correct," Simon added, looking smug.

"Yeah right, Burrow. Robin Hood was just a story. People are too self-centered to worry about society," Jamie commented before taking a sip from the mug of beer.

"On the contrary, our thief seems to be the exception. Check this out," Burrows replied, pushing a file toward Jamie and opening up to the papers inside.

"What's this? How the hell did you figure this out?" Jamie asked.

"I'm good at my job, Jamie. You should take a few pointers from me."

"Good at your job? This must have been some kind of lucky guess."

"Well, the bills match. Who would have known that Chico Santez would mark every bill before doing a drug exchange?"

"Yeah, that's pretty damn smart. So whoever stole the money during the drug deal donated twenty thousand of it to the children's burn unit after they were robbed only ten thousand? Sounds like a modern day Robin Hood to me," Detective Burrow replied.

"Yeah, except where is the forty thousand left over?" Jamie asked.

"Robin Hood's payoff for a job well done," Donny replied from the corner of the room.

"Or how about some other small contributions along the way? Like the food shelter that was robbed last year or the day care program that was going to get cut? Could be the same person or could be different people," Burrows added with a smile.

"Does it really matter anyway? Drugs are being taken off the streets, and good people are receiving money. I personally don't have a problem with that. Let's talk about bringing down Bret, Carlos, Chico, and the rest of these scumbags by the book, so Robin Hood can retire," Donny stated, and everyone laughed.

* * * *

Melissa felt her stomach begin to ache and her palms sweat. Oh shit, she never thought that Chico would mark bills. Who the hell did that?

She tried to remain relaxed, as if their conversation bored her or that she wasn't listening, but suddenly she began to shake and asked herself why she had accepted this gig.

* * * *

"I think we need another informant. Someone who can get on the inside or at least keep us amidst of any new information that can help us put Chico, Carlos, Bret, and the Fernandez family behind bars," Jamie suggested, and then he looked toward Melissa.

She was always so bright, and he knew she had been trying to achieve her law degree until Mike and Sarah died. At one point, she had a fling with Bret, which was over before Jamie had time to reprimand her and warn her. Thank God, or she could have wound up dead.

They continued to talk about some new information they had and about organizing a sting once the laboratory was located and confirmed.

Twenty minutes later they were preparing for dinner.

* * * *

Melissa was nervous and anxious for this night to end. Although she kept telling herself that there was no way the cops would find out it was her who committed the hits, she was still concerned. She hoped that they didn't know that she knew Bret.

"Hey, Melissa, grab something to eat. You've been here all night," Jamie stated as he brought her a plate of food.

"I'm good."

"Eat something," he suggested, but she sensed an almost order in his tone. The fact he had a sidearm and his badge hanging on his waist was intimidation for her, so she walked around the bar and joined him and the others at the table.

They ate in silence, and soon the guys were having their own conversations, and Jamie spoke with her.

He took a forkful of chicken marsala and asked her a question before eating it.

"How's that law degree coming along?"

She swallowed her mouthful of salad and shrugged her shoulders. She almost felt as if he were reprimanding her.

"Don't tell me you quit trying to get it?"

"No, I just kind of had to put it all on hold."

"You'd make a great attorney. Especially a prosecuting attorney. We could use your help to put away scumbags like Bret."

She swallowed hard and tried to act nonchalant.

"Who?"

He took a sip of beer and held her gaze. His interrogating expression caught her off guard.

"I know you know who Bret is, honey. I'm just glad you got uninvolved with him as quickly as you got involved with him."

She placed her fork down on the plate and clasped her hands on her lap, and Jamie reached over and covered her knee with his hand. "Hey, I was worried about you when I found out, but the second I heard you dumped the asshole I was relieved. It's got to be tough, struggling with money, trying to take care of an instant family, and your sick aunt while working around men like Bret. You know, all that 'fuck you' money and shit."

She held his gaze. "It was a mistake, but it was over quick. I fell for his good looks and exceptional charms. He sweet-talked me, and I was in a fragile state at the time. I'm only human, Jamie," she added. He intimidated her but he also put her on edge. Who was he to reprimand her life or her actions? She didn't want to make a scene or argue with him, but her gut instincts were pulling hard. Perhaps it was due to the conversation about Robin Hood earlier?

He squeezed her knee and moved closer to her so he could whisper.

"I know that. I've thought about you a lot, and I knew you were busy taking care of things. Hell, I left you messages to call me, but you never did. Why not?" he asked, sounding sad.

"I'm sorry about that, Jamie, but I've had very little time to myself. It's still like that now. Look where I am. I never met Paul before tonight. I've never heard of this men's club or this private party room, yet this is the kind of work I need to do to survive. I'm just trying to survive, Jamie." Just then her cell phone buzzed again.

He leaned back into his chair and eyed her cell as she glanced at the number.

"That's some overprotective boyfriend you got," he teased, but she knew that look. He was jealous and almost angry. She might as well pretend and get Jamie off her case.

"Yeah, well, I'm not sure if I want him to be my boyfriend."

His jaw tightened and his nostrils flared as he inhaled then exhaled heavily.

"Why's that?"

She thought for a moment, and the brothers popped into her head then she replied.

"He's real big and muscular. It kind of intimidates me."

"He's not rough with you, is he?" he asked with concern then slowly took her wrist into his hand, slightly separating the black bracelets she wore, revealing her bruised wrist.

She pulled it out of his grasp.

"No. He most definitely isn't." She attempted to stand up, but Jamie stopped her, placing his hands on the arms of the chair she sat in.

"How is Charlie's place working out for you? I hear he has some regular clientele with big bucks supporting the club."

And so it began. He was looking for information.

"If you wanted information, then why did Paul go through all this work to create a job for me? I can't help you," she stated then shoved his hands away and rose from the seat. By now the rest of the conversations had halted, and everyone was listening to them.

"What is she talking about, Jamie? I didn't make up this job for her."

Melissa looked at Paul then back at Justin.

"I think my job here is over, Paul. Can you pay up so I can leave?"

"Melissa works at Charlie's. Bret, Chico, and Carlos were in there last night. She was tending bar for their private party."

They all looked at her, but she raised her chin and crossed her arms in front of her chest.

"Is this true, Melissa? You know the men we were just discussing?" Paul asked.

"I know who they are, and yes, I was tending bar last night for their little party. I don't have any information for you. Nothing was discussed."

"I heard it got pretty intense around three o'clock or so."

Melissa knew she looked guilty of something, but they had no evidence, no proof at all. This was hearsay and no specifics. Jamie and the rest of these cops would have to do better than this to get her to rat out gangsters and drug dealers. If she said a word, her family was as good as dead.

"What happened, Melissa?" the lieutenant asked.

She was quiet for a few seconds and contemplated the story she would give them.

"It got a little crazy at the end. Bret had too much to drink. He thought he could buy me, too," she said then held her wrist, rubbing it with her good hand.

Justin reached over and took it into his hand, looking it over.

"He did this to you?"

She nodded.

"If Charlie and Spike, the bouncer, didn't break through the door, it would have been a lot worse."

"Shit, Melissa. When Bret wants something, he gets it. No one says no or they end up dead."

He touched her cheek then trailed a finger across her chin near her neck.

"What about this?" He questioned the makeup she used to cover up the slight bruising on her chin and cheek. That was a shock, waking up to that this morning and then hiding it from her aunt and the kids.

"I said it got a little crazy."

"What conversation went on in that room?" the lieutenant asked.

"I told you, nothing. They were there to party, get drunk, and bullshit."

"Melissa, if you have information that can help us put Bret and the others behind bars, you need to tell me. We'll protect you."

She pulled away from him and took a step away.

"You can't protect my family. I don't know anything, and if I did, I wouldn't say a word. I need money to support the kids and my aunt. If I lose that job, I'm finished."

She walked away and back toward the bar.

* * * *

Jamie walked out of the room and exhaled. He couldn't believe what he heard. He knew Melissa, and she was aware of information in regards to the drug dealing and perhaps the locations of labs they were looking for. She was just scared.

He glanced down at her cell phone.

He pulled it from her hip when she abruptly rose from the chair. He felt shitty for doing it, but he wanted to know who was calling her. If she was privy to information and had chosen to work as a bartender for private parties, then she knew stuff. Friend or not, the department was desperate to catch Bret and these other men. He looked at the numbers and the texts she received. This couldn't be right. He checked the numbers again and then confirmed it. How the hell did she know Logan and his brothers? Justin felt conflicted. He knew the other Valdamars, Logan's cousins, Dustin, Kyle, Adam, Trey, and Donny. Frankie's text mentioned needing to kiss her again. Was she fucking him? Was it possible that she was with all of them? He was jealous and envious at the same time. The Valdamar brothers were some serious men. They were huge, and they were not men to fuck around with. What the hell was going on? They were involved with this case as well. It would be their team infiltrating the drug laboratory and operations building once the information was confirmed. Did the Valdamar brothers know that Melissa was at that meeting last night at the club? Do they know Bret attacked her?

He had a moral dilemma here. Dustin had saved his ass last year during a drug raid gone bad. Logan and his brothers were good men and had always pulled through for the department. Why was Melissa avoiding their calls?

Taking a deep breath, he closed her phone and walked back into the room. She was cleaning up the bar preparing to leave. Paul was paying her.

Nonchalantly Jamie walked over to the table and sat down, staring at Melissa as he inconspicuously dropped her cell phone under the chair she had been sitting in.

"Good luck, Melissa. Be safe," Paul stated as he shook her hand and thanked her for her service tonight. The other men were walking out the door, and it was just Paul and Jamie now.

"Hey, let's keep in touch. Don't be such a stranger," Jamie stated.

"You want to keep in touch as a friend or as a detective investigating a case and looking for a snitch?" she asked with attitude.

"A friend of, course. Give me your cell number so we can talk sometime."

He watched as the panic hit her face as she realized her cell was missing. He played dumb and watched as she searched on the floor behind the bar then around the bar.

"Hey, I think I see something under the table," Paul stated, reaching down to the floor. He pulled out the cell phone.

"Looks like you got another text."

She grabbed it from him. "Thanks."

He said good-bye as she grabbed her bag and left the room.

* * * *

Melissa couldn't wait to get the hell out of there. It was nearly midnight when she received the call from Celine.

The text said urgent, so she called her the second she got into her car.

"What's going on?"

"I'm in trouble, Mel. I'm in serious fucking trouble."

"What trouble? What's going on? Are the kids okay?" she asked in a panic.

"Yes, the kids are fine. They're in the other room sleeping, and so is your aunt. I heard from the bank, and because I wouldn't fuck that little weasel that came to the apartment the other day, he messed with my records. They say I owe ninety thousand dollars, Mel. Where the hell am I going to get that kind of money? The bank called and said if I don't have it by tomorrow or make a payment of at least half of it, they'll arrest me. They'll take my kids, Mel, they'll take my kids." Celine cried hysterically.

"Damn it, Celine. Maybe we can get a lawyer?"

"And pay for it how? Can't you see that it wouldn't matter? There's no time, Mel. I'm going to jail, and I am going to lose my kids."

Melissa was scrambling for a solution. There had to be a way around this. Maybe she could go talk to the bank guy and make him change the numbers back? Maybe she could get help from the police or maybe Jamie? No, if she did he would probably ask for her help to bring down Bret. She couldn't do that. She had to handle this alone. Just like all the other times.

"Watch the kids for me. Don't panic if you don't hear from me right away. I'll fix this, Celine. I promise."

* * * *

Melissa felt her heart beating so fast she thought she would pass out. Desperate times called for desperate measures. That's exactly what she kept telling herself.

She kept her back to the concrete wall inside the building. If she had gotten the call from Celine an hour earlier, she could have better prepared herself for this hit. Melissa remembered Bret saying something about Lester Crowe meeting a guy and trading the drugs for money. She almost missed his black sports car as it sped down Fifth and Madison Avenue. She continued to follow him, all the way through Harlem and on to the road leading to an old warehouse. Parking her car three blocks away, near a bodega, she sprinted on foot through the dark alleyways to get here on time. Now, the little shit was nowhere in sight. If she could see who he was meeting then get the money, Celine would be in the clear.

Her insides fluttered with trepidation. This was not a well-planned attack. This was desperation. When people got desperate, they screwed up. She fought with her conscious over leaving now before something went wrong or coming through for her best friend. She couldn't live with herself if something happened to Celine or the kids.

She had experienced foster care for a short period of time as a kid. It wasn't an experience she told anyone about. She wouldn't allow the babies to be sent there. She just couldn't. Plus she had experienced twenty-four hours in jail. Celine was weak and easy prey. The people in jail would eat her alive.

Melissa convinced herself to get through this. Get the money and run. Fix Celine's problems and be finished forever. This was going to be her last hit for good.

She wasn't concerned about Bret or his men losing such money. It would all be on Lester and the other guy anyway. Both were pigs and scumbags. Especially when it came to women.

She slowly made her way around each corner then to the meeting location.

No one was around until she saw two men dressed in white smoking cigarettes by a door near a building next door to where she was.

She wondered what they were up to because she knew that building was abandoned.

A sound caught her attention, and she saw Lester and the other guy.

Lester had a huge bag, and so did the other dude she didn't recognize.

Taking soft, quick steps, she made her way around their position and took her position between a small entryway that divided the building where the two men dressed in white had been moments ago. They went back inside the doorway.

Lester chitchatted with the some Spanish guy, and she wondered why he was taking so long. Lester was an idiot. In a delivery you hurry up. Get in and out as quickly as possible. No small talk. The Spanish guy appeared concerned, but Lester kept talking.

Then it ended as the Spanish guy took over.

"Let's do this. I got plans," he stated. They switched bags, and the Spanish guy disappeared down the alleyway.

Lester placed the bag on the ground and stood there waiting.

What the hell is he waiting for? Come this way, moron. Just a few feet.

Melissa was losing her patience when she saw what he had waited for. Pulling up his sleeve, she watched as he wrapped the piece of rubber around his upper arm then knelt on the ground.

The bag was now behind him.

Is he serious? He's going to give himself a hit right here?

She watched in disbelief as he got the needle ready and injected himself. His head rolled back, and he fell to his ass on the ground.

Dumb fucking idiot. Drugs rule your life then eventually kill you. This was just the scenario she needed.

In a flash, she ran toward him to grab the bag. He turned haphazardly and grabbed at her arm, but she fought him off. He wouldn't know it was her. She wore a mask, and he was nearly out of it. They wrestled a bit, but she was able to get free from his grasp as the drugs hit his system. She took the bag and ran like hell away from the scene. Lester was still in a daze because she never heard him following.

She had a funny feeling and decided to check the bag. She didn't want to grab the drugs. She wanted the cash. She knelt down and unzipped the bag. Bingo. A shitload of dough.

As she stood up and headed toward the alleyway, she saw the multiple sets of vehicles, slowly making their way past where she was and toward the building next door.

Her stomach felt as if it dropped. Cops! Oh, crap.

She ran as fast as she could and toward the block where her car was. A quick glance over her shoulder and she saw the SWAT team vehicle and the sound of gunfire. She nearly cried out in terror, almost losing her breath from the fear that grasped her heart.

She was too close for comfort, too, and prayed she wouldn't get caught. What if it were the brothers? What would they do if they caught her?

The sounds of gunfire continued to echo nearby. She heard numerous sirens as more police cruisers came onto the scene just yards from where she stood. Her mouth suddenly became too dry to swallow. Her heart pounded against her chest with fear. If she got caught, everyone she cared for would suffer. Celine would wind up in jail, the babies in foster care, and her own kids would suffer immensely. They couldn't handle losing another loved one. Melissa saw her car and jumped inside just as a police car came up the same avenue. She ducked down low.

They paid no attention to her and thankfully she got out of there.

* * * *

Melissa separated the money and hid it in Celine's apartment. She called her and told her where it was and what to do tomorrow morning. She signed a deposit slip for the checking account. That way Celine would have the money available and show the bank that she was able to pay off the debt. When Melissa had the opportunity, she would pay that little bank weasel a visit and set his ass straight. If things went well, then Celine would have a large bank account in no time. The kids would be safe, and Celine could calm down so she could straighten out her life.

She took a quick shower, changed her clothes, and placed the stuff she wore to Paul's back on then headed out to her car.

* * * *

Logan was stationed inside the command center. They had planned this raid for two weeks. Once the informant explained to the lieutenant where this small meth lab was located, they knew it would be a big hit to Bret and his operation. Logan, Sunny, Frankie, Vince, and Jake were looking forward to taking Bret and the others down, especially after what Bret had tried with Melissa. When Simon

Burrow called him a couple of hours ago and mentioned Melissa's possible involvement with information on Bret, he and his brothers were pissed off. They were willing to give up this raid to team three and head after Melissa. But Burrow talked them out of it. He informed them that she was heading home for the night and where she had been. They were relieved that she was okay but unhappy that she hadn't contacted them.

In an instant, his brothers had the door slammed down and the place filled with smoke bombs and fake explosions. The shock-and-awe approach always worked in these types of situations.

Twenty minutes later and they had forty-two men and women under arrest and a successful raid accomplished.

As they did a sweep of the surrounding buildings, Jake notified Logan through his headset that he found someone.

"I got one drugged out asshole in cuffs. He's flying high and carrying on about money missing and being a dead man."

"Do you recognize him?" Logan asked.

"No, but that's the least of my worries. He's a skull head."

"Then what's the problem? Just bring him in."

"The main problem is that I smell our mate," Jake stated through what sounded like clenched teeth.

Logan's own temper began to rise.

"On him?" Frankie asked, joining the conversation and sounding about ready to roar.

"No. But she was here. I found a bracelet, too. It smells like her. It's hers."

"What the fuck was she doing there?"

"I think we need to bring her in, Logan. Burrow could be onto something. She's a potential suspect. She could be involved with all of this," Jake said.

Logan felt his brothers' emotions. They were all angry, concerned, and wondered if their mate was involved with drug dealing and with Bret.

"Give the skull to one of the patrol officers and get back here. Our job is done, and we need to find Melissa," Logan stated, and they all hurried back to the truck.

* * * *

Melissa was exhausted as she jumped into the car to head back home. She was slowly starting to relax. It was done. She made it, and now Celine would be fine. The babies would have their mother, and Melissa would be finished with doing hits on the bad guys. She had written out four separate deposit slips and precise plans for Celine to follow to break down the money so there would be no way of tracing it. She hoped Celine could handle it.

She pulled her car into the parking spot and turned off the ignition. As she exited her car, she heard a sound, and in an instant her body was pressed against the car and her legs spread.

"Put your hands on the vehicle and spread your legs!" Jake ordered, pressing his thick, hard body against her back, forcing her legs open and her hands up against the metal of the car.

"What's going on? What did I do?" she asked, her cracking voice giving away her instant fear. She was terrified. They caught her. They knew what she did.

He frisked her, being thorough as he pressed under her breasts to the metal wire, then between her legs and against her pussy and inner thighs.

Holy shit, she was panting, and did she just moan?

"Is she clean?" a voice asked, and she tried to turn to see who it was, but Frankie held her hair and pressed his face against her cheek. He inhaled then whispered.

"I think further investigation is needed, sir," he responded, like some trained soldier taking a command from his leader. She wasn't frightened, in fact she was utterly turned on by their power and control. She was guilty, but they had yet to explain why they were arresting her. As intimidating and turned on as she was, she needed to remain in control here.

She saw Jake as he quickly searched her vehicle. She was smarter than that. She wouldn't leave any evidence or money in her car, especially since she knew that Chico marked his money and that maybe Bret did the same.

Swiftly Frankie placed her hands behind her back and cuffed her. The cool, hard metal wasn't so foreign to her. It brought back unhappy thoughts as she felt the tears roll down her cheeks. She was shocked at her own body's unconscious reaction.

"Please don't hurt me. I'll cooperate," she begged as Frankie turned her toward him. She saw the gleam in his eye as well as a hint of compassion. She hoped that's what it was.

"No can do. We're taking you in. We're getting to the bottom of this."

Chapter 9

They placed her into the black vehicle that looked like a combination of a van and a truck. As Frankie lifted her up, Vince took her from him as if she weighed nothing at all.

He gave her a disappointed and angry look, so she put her head down as he placed her on a seat. Vince strapped her, being sure to be gentle as he caressed her arms and rechecked her handcuffs, making sure that they weren't too snug, then he took a seat beside her. The others were there. She felt them and somehow knew they were all watching her.

"Why are you doing this?" she asked as she slowly lifted her head up. The interior was dark. She could hardly see their faces, but she did see their eyes. Three sets of gold watched her, and an eerie feeling filled her heart.

They were silent, and it bothered her so much to think that they hated her or were disgusted with her. They were strangers. They were men she was sexually attracted to, but she hadn't given in to their lustful pursuit. At least Celine had the children and they had enough money if Melissa went to jail. She sighed as she thought about what these men were going to do. If she kept her mouth shut, they would never find out about the hits.

A while later, just as she started to wonder why they weren't at one of the precincts where they could book her then question her before sending her to a cell for the night, Sunny spoke.

"This is how it is going to go down, little dancer. We're going to get to the bottom of all this secrecy, and you are going to answer all of our questions. If you lie, if you keep anything from us, there'll be punishments. Do you understand?"

She heard the authority and determination in his voice and knew she wouldn't stand a chance with these men. They were more than men. They were wolves that could kill her in a snap.

She nodded just as the vehicle came to a halt.

* * * *

Logan pulled the vehicle into the garage and turned off the lights. This building was separate from their home. It stood a few hundred feet away from the main house.

This was where they worked on their training, developed and improved their weapons, and mentally prepared for the various missions they were sent on for the government.

One look at Melissa and the tight, sexy outfit she wore to work at Paul's place made Sunny's dick hard. He thought there could be better ways to get the truth from Melissa besides talking. Like maybe a good old-fashioned ass spanking. It was a possibility, considering she wore a short black miniskirt that showed off her luscious ass, but then there was also the midriff-cut top that revealed her perfect abs. That was enough to send him over the edge. Add in the handcuffs and yeah, he wanted to bend her over the workbench and fuck the truth out of her. But then there was the fact that Melissa was their mate. His wolf wanted to protect her, love her, and keep her safe. What better way than to find out what she was involved in and how deep. If it turned out that she in fact was selling drugs, he and his brothers would have a lot to figure out.

He watched as Logan pressed her body into a folding chair then turned on the bright overhanging light.

He leaned on the table directly in front of her and stared at her.

"Where were you tonight?"

They watched her swallow hard then blink her eyes. Those beautiful, brown doe eyes looked so sad and frightened, but they had to do this.

"What?'

"You heard him, now answer!" Frankie yelled at her, making her adjust her ass in the seat. The skirt was so tight Sunny could practically see all the way up it. That's when Melissa crossed her legs. How could she be so ladylike when she wore such a "fuck-me" outfit?

"I was working at a new place for a guy named Paul."

Logan eyed her body, and when she inhaled, her breasts pressed forward, and the men stared directly at them Her nipples hardened. Was their little dancer getting turned on from being restrained? Interesting.

"What kind of work?"

"Bartending, nothing more," she replied with just a hint of attitude.

"What time did you leave there?"

She hesitated, and they knew she was trying to hide the truth.

"What time? Answer him," Vince demanded this time.

Her doe eyes shot to him then back to Logan.

"Eleven, I think."

Logan abruptly pulled her chair forward, making her body jerk and her legs uncross.

"You think?" he reprimanded.

She moved her wrists behind her back and tilted her chin up in defiance.

"I don't recall."

Logan stared at her. He could hear her heart beat faster as he reached forward and touched her chin. He gently ran a finger down her neck then over the thin material of the revealing top she wore.

He continued to hold her gaze as he ran his finger softly over the material covering her right nipple. Instantly it hardened from his touch, and her luscious lips parted in a soft gasp. He never released her gaze. He saw the glazed-over look and the sultry way her body eased lower in the chair. So he reached over and trailed his finger over her left breast and nipple doing the same thing.

"Is this some sort of sex game? Did you kidnap me and think that I would be turned on by this?"

He chuckled lightly at her abrupt question.

"This isn't a game, and we didn't kidnap you. You're under arrest."

"This is not proper protocol."

"Spoken like someone who knows the drill," Frankie stated from behind her.

She swallowed hard. "Am I under arrest?" she asked through clenched teeth.

In an instant, Logan grabbed a fistful of her shirt, lifted her from the chair and pressed her body against the wall behind her. The sound of the chair falling to the floor echoed through the room. She jumped as he thrust his hips low against her crotch, lifting her feet from the floor.

With her hands cuffed behind her, she had no choice but to allow him to balance her.

"I'll ask all the questions, and you will answer them."

He heard her heart beat faster, and her breath collided with his neck.

He whispered to her with teeth practically clenched.

"Are you working for Bret?"

She was scared, he could tell, but she was tough.

She shook her head.

"Are you fucking him?" Logan felt his eyes glow and knew it scared Melissa, but he wanted the truth.

"No," she stated firmly and filled with attitude.

He pushed her skirt up so he could adjust her legs so that they straddled his hips. That way he could hold her better so he wouldn't hurt her arms.

Rubbing the palms of his hands across her naked ass cheeks, he wondered if she wasn't wearing underwear. After further investigation with his finger, brushing it along her crevice, he felt the string of her thong underwear.

"If you're not fucking Bret and you're not working for him, then what the fuck were you doing at his warehouse tonight?"

He saw her facial coloring change to almost white and then her struggle to get free. He smelled her fear and gripped her tighter in preparation of a struggle.

"Let me go! Damn it, let me down," she demanded. She twisted and pulled in his arms, and Logan held her tighter as he pulled away from the wall.

"What were you doing there?" Frankie asked, determined to know Melissa's involvement.

"I wasn't there!" she hollered.

"Then what the fuck is this?" Frankie asked as he held up the black bracelet to her face.

She was hesitant then whispered, "I don't know."

Frankie went behind her and undid the handcuffs. He pulled her wrist in front of her, showing the set of matching bracelets still on her wrist.

She was quick with her reaction.

"That could be anyone's bracelet. I wasn't there. I don't know where his warehouse is, and you can't prove anything."

Frankie's eyes began to glow, and Logan knew his brother was losing control.

Frankie sniffed the bracelet, and then he moved forward, sniffing Melissa's neck.

He took his time inhaling then licking her skin. Melissa couldn't fight Frankie's assault. He was omitting the mating musk to weaken her defenses.

"I smell you on the bracelet. Jake smelled your scent at the scene and on the dirtbag we arrested."

Sam opened her eyes to look at Frankie then Jake. "You're wrong. You made a mistake."

"Wolves don't make mistakes."

Slowly Logan released Melissa, letting her stand back on her own two feet.

He held her hands against his chest with one hand while his other arm held her around the waist.

"Wolves are never wrong. We know you were there. Now tell the truth."

She slowly shook her head.

* * * *

Melissa felt the tears reach her eyes. She couldn't tell them why she was really there. They would make her hand over the money, and everything she did for Celine and the babies would have been a waste and not worth the risk.

The tears rolled down her cheeks. "I can't."

Logan squeezed her tighter as she heard Frankie's gasp of annoyance with her. Vince, Sunny, and Jake were leaning against some workbench just staring at her.

"Why can't you, Melissa? If you're in some kind of trouble, we'll help you," Vince added. She felt his sincerity but couldn't trust him. She couldn't let her body make a decision that could ruin the lives of her loved ones.

She had to lie. For the sake of Celine's kids, her Aunt Peggy, and her sister's kids, she had no choice.

"I met an old friend at Paul's place tonight. He's doing an investigation into Bret's involvement with illegal drugs. He asked for my help, and I denied him at the club but then felt compelled to help."

She watched as they eyed her suspiciously.

"Why would you risk your life for some old friend?"

She felt the shitty feeling inside before the words left her lips.

"Because he was a good friend of my sister and brother-in-law's. They died in a drive-by shooting because of drug dealers."

* * * *

"Either she's a really good liar or she was really that stupid enough to go to the warehouse on her own," Frankie stated.

"But what about the guy? Why would her scent be on the guy if she wasn't in direct contact with him?" Logan countered.

"If that's true, Melissa, then how come the guy Jake arrested had your scent on him?" Logan asked.

Melissa lowered her head then exhaled.

"I know Lester Crowe. He's the one you arrested. I was talking to him, trying to get some information because Bret always sends Lester on stupid errands. He's a good resource of information," Melissa told them.

"And how do you know this?" Sunny asked.

"Lester would show up at Charlie's whenever Bret was around."

Logan grabbed her arm and pulled her against his chest.

"Sounds like you know Bret pretty damn well. How is that, Melissa, and don't tell me it's from bartending and observing him."

"I went out with him once, is that what you want to hear? I was stupid and I fell for his charms and his sexy good looks, okay, Logan."

Melissa tried to pull away from Logan, but he wouldn't release her.

"You dated him long?" Logan asked.

"Yeah, and I fucked him, too, so let me go. You've got nothing on me and nothing to hold me in a court of law, so release me now, Logan," she demanded.

Logan felt his eyes change.

"Don't push me, Melissa."

She shoved against his chest.

Logan couldn't take it any longer. Being this close to his mate, inhaling her scent and tolerating her defiance was too much for his wolf. He pulled her against his chest and covered her mouth in a lethal kiss.

Melissa protested at first and then fought for control of the kiss.

Things got out of control quickly as Logan lifted Melissa by her ass cheeks and pressed her onto the table. He spread her legs with his thighs and hips then sheltered her head and neck between his forearms as he continued to ravage her mouth.

Melissa was rubbing her hands all over his body, trying to press him harder against her.

He explored her mouth, tasting her as his need to fuck his mate began to increase.

When he felt Melissa grab his ass and squeeze as she thrust her hips against his, that was it.

Slowly, Logan released her lips and continued to suck on her neck.

Melissa grabbed for his shirt, trying to remove it from his body.

"Fuck, Melissa, I'm not going to stop. I want you too fucking badly to stop right now and interrogate your ass." He growled as he cupped her breast and rubbed his other hand over her thigh, pushing up her skirt.

"Then stop being a cop and just fuck me already. I can't take this ache inside. I need you," she pleaded.

* * * *

Melissa never felt so desperate, and her body never felt this hot and needy. There was something about these men that turned her on and turned her mind upside down.

The fact that they were cops and could bust her for her illegal pastime was a total turn-on. Then, of course, there were their bodies. Logan was built like a linebacker with his thick waist and even thicker cock. Her pussy dripped with desire the moment he asked her if she was fucking Bret. Bret was a huge mistake, and right now she hoped she wasn't making an even greater mistake.

"I'm not going to be able to go slow this time, Melissa. I'm too wound up." Logan growled as he lifted her hips up higher, pushing her skirt to her waist.

* * * *

Logan caught scent of her arousal. Her panties were soaked, and the sight of the tiny, thin, black thong that barely covered his mate's cunt was hot.

"Fuck yeah," he stated then rubbed his nose against her pussy as he lifted her legs to his shoulders.

Melissa gasped for air as she grabbed his head and thrust her pussy up against his face.

He pulled back only slightly to rip the material from her body.

Her pussy lips sparkled with desire, and he couldn't wait to taste her cream. He licked her from ass to cunt loving the taste of her. Melissa grabbed a hold of his hair and thrust up against his mouth as he plunged his tongue inside her pussy.

Pulling out, he felt his wolf come alive inside of him.

"She tastes incredible. Hold her arms. She likes being bound, isn't that right, Mel?" Logan commanded.

She moaned as his brothers assisted. "Yes," she stated, pushing her chest out as Logan flicked his tongue at her wet folds.

Her cream was like nothing he ever tasted before. It was sweet and tangy as he played with her labia, being sure to lick every bit of her. He saw Frankie grab her arms and pull her shirt from her body.

"We're going to show you how good it's going to be with us, Melissa. You belong to us," Frankie said.

Logan pressed two fingers to her pussy lips, spreading them wider so he could take another taste. Melissa moaned and pleaded for more.

"Please, Logan. Please don't tease me."

He looked up at her body, from her slick pussy lips to her belly ring against toned abs all the way to her abundant breasts. She was perfect.

He pressed two fingers in and out of her pussy, and Melissa began to thrust against his fist.

"You want my cock, Mel. Tell me how much you need it," he teased her as she rolled her head side to side.

"I want it. I need it," she panted.

Logan unzipped his pants then reached to her skirt, pulling it down and out of the way.

She was bare to all of them, and his brothers inhaled their mate's scent.

"She smells fantastic," Sunny commented.

* * * *

Melissa was in sexual stimulation overload as Logan finger-fucked her, licking her cream while his brothers watched.

Frankie unclasped her bra and ripped it from her body, tossing it as he leaned forward with his mouth and licked her nipple.

He cupped her left breast as he licked and tasted every inch as if it were food.

Vince took her right breast into his mouth and did the same thing.

She never thought about having sex with more than one person before. She was shocked at her body's reaction and the desire to fuck all five of these sexy men. She tried to reach for them, to touch their sensational bodies. As her fingers touched Logan's shoulders her pussy wept. He was solid muscle and it was a total turn-on.

"Get ready, baby, I'm giving you what you want." Logan fisted his cock in his hand and held her gaze.

The man was gifted in the cock department. His significant size made her tighten in his hold and close her eyes.

Surprisingly, Logan took his time. He must have read her facial expression.

Inch by inch, he pushed his cock into her pussy as Vince and Frankie pulled on her nipples and sucked them.

She moaned as the full feeling enveloped her core. Looking down, she was shocked that Logan wasn't fully inside of her.

"Oh god, Logan!" she moaned.

He lifted her thighs and shoved forward, taking her breath away.

So much for going slow. With every thrust she felt his cock somehow grow harder and thicker.

All she could do was hold on as Logan took over fucking her as he licked her nipples then her neck.

"You feel so tight, Melissa, so fucking tight."

Over and over again he thrust his hips, pounding his cock into her pussy, sending her into multiple orgasms. She felt the hard wood at her back and the way Logan's heavy body pressed her to it. She was incredibly turned on. She felt wild with need as she ran her hands over every part of his body she could reach. His muscles shifted beneath her palms as she squeezed and scratched at him with each of his thrusts.

When she noticed Logan's distorted expression, she knew he was about to come inside of her and the panic hit her.

"Protection! We forgot protection."

"None needed. We're clean, Melissa. You're ours, and we will always protect you," Logan growled as he increased his thrusts fast and hard until he exploded inside of her.

* * * *

Melissa tried to catch her breath and come to terms with what Logan just said. She didn't know shit about wolves, just what she had picked up on with the men. They seemed possessive immediately of her. Did they think that they owned her?

Before she could question them, Logan was pulling out of her then pulling her up from the table and into his arms.

He kissed her lips then her neck as he nuzzled her body against his. His shoulder-length hair tapped against her cheeks as she held on tight.

"Let's get you to the house. We need a bed."

Someone wrapped a blanket over her shoulders before Logan carried her from the building.

Chapter 10

"What the fuck do you mean you smelled Mel on Lester?" Bret asked Deatrix as he held the other wolf by his collar about to choke him to death.

Deatrix's eyes widened in fear of his alpha, his leader's wrath.

"I smelled her scent on Lester when I paid his bail and got him out of the holding cell."

"Are you saying that my Mel was fucking Lester the crackhead?"

"No, sir. I'm saying she was there last night in the alley. She had contact with him before the raid."

Bret released Deatrix abruptly then turned around, thinking about this new information.

"Could she be dealing on the side? Maybe making a few extra bucks behind my back?"

"I don't know, and Lester was too high on 'meth' to remember anything. I can ask around and see if she's dealing?" Deatrix suggested.

"Do that, and call Charlie to find out when Mel is working again."

Deatrix left the office, and Bret thought about this new information.

There was some new guy trying to make a name for himself dealing drugs. He had some different suppliers and connections than Bret, Carlos, and Chico knew of. Perhaps Mel was getting her shit from him. It was a question he would have to ask her next time he saw Mel. He was definitely going to see her again. His wolf got a hold of her scent, and no other pussy was doing it for him.

He hit the intercom and asked Chu to come into his office.

A few seconds later, Chu arrived.

"I want you to find out if Mel is dealing drugs with the new supplier, Miguel. I don't like him, and I sure as hell don't want him around Mel."

"Don't you think you should lay low for a while with Mel's boss?"

"Fuck no. She's going to be my woman whether she accepts that willingly or not."

Chu nodded then headed out the door.

* * * *

Detective Jamie Montgomery walked into the police department and right to Lieutenant Sparks's office.

"So what do we got, Jamie?" the lieutenant asked.

Jamie closed the office door and stood a few feet away from the Lieutenant's desk.

"The dumb shit we picked up doesn't remember anything. He should be coming down from his high soon. You should see the track marks on this asshole," Jamie stated, sounding disgusted.

"Yeah, well, what I don't understand is how someone who appears to be as smart as Bret Wilcox would let some lowlife asshole like Lester Crowe run a drug exchange that big. The street value of the shit we took off the other asshole was worth eighty thousand at least. How much fucking money was stolen from Lester anyway?"

"I have no fucking idea. My guess would be over a hundred grand."

"What's the possibility that this was a planned hit, and what's the possibility that it was some lucky robber's great night?" the lieutenant asked.

"Everyone on the streets knows that the neighborhood belongs to Bret. There are very few willing to cross him, and this is a lot of money. The word on the street was that this was an outside job.

Someone quick, aware of the drug business and how Bret works," Jamie replied.

"Oh, great. Another person fucking Bret over secretively?"

"Could be. I really wish we could get Melissa to help us out here. I bet she could find out who stole this money and where that huge drug lab is located."

"She seemed adamant about involving herself in it, Jamie. I'm sure she regrets getting involved with Bret at one time. I liked her, and she seemed like a good kid."

"She needs a little incentive. I'll work on her and see if I can get her to help out."

"Well, Detective Burrow thinks she could be of some help if persuaded. Sounds good. So how about the raid from SWAT team one? I heard they were fucking faster than lightning and had the place secured in a matter of minutes."

"They have quite the reputation. You mess with them and you're going down. They did a great job. It was Jake Valdamar that located Lester and arrested him."

"Excellent. We'll definitely use them the next time around. Where are you off to now?"

"A few leads on last night's robber and then off to see Melissa and her aunt."

"Good luck with that," the lieutenant stated then smirked.

Jamie gave him an irritated look then left the office.

Chapter 11

Melissa's breasts were pressed against Logan's chest, her arms wrapped around his neck, as his arms held her underneath her ass. She kept her legs wrapped around him best she could, but without his strong arms holding her, she would slide off. He was thick around the waist, and her legs weren't long enough to cross behind him. She absorbed the feel of his arms of steel and the beat of his heart as their skin connected. Melissa felt highly in tune to every sensation, every emotion and presence around her.

She felt Logan's long, thick cock tap against her ass as he walked across the grass. Her mound was pressed against his muscular abs and only added to her sexual stimulation. This odd vibration hummed through her body. She was acutely aware that the others followed close behind and she somehow sensed their need to have sex with her, too. It was crazy. She was going to do this. She wanted a piece of all of them. Then suddenly her thoughts changed. They were awfully quiet. No one said a word and one glance over Logan's shoulder and she saw their glowing eyes and their serious facial expressions. She clenched her eyes tightly before taking another peek.

She tried to see where he was going and hoped that he wasn't headed into the woods to shift into a wolf and make her run for her life. The thought brought on a surge of fear. She could just imagine their elongated teeth, sharp claws, and deep ferocious howls coming after her as she ran naked through the woods like their prey. It was not an appealing thought.

A glance up from Logan's shoulder and she saw the others following close behind Logan. Their eyes still glowed, and their faces held expressions of anger and hunger. Unconsciously, she clung tighter to Logan, and he noticed.

"Why are you shaking?" he asked.

"I'm not shaking," she tried to reply with an attitude, but her words were shaky to even her own ears.

"Sure you are. I can sense your fear, Melissa."

"Where are you taking me?"

"Where do you think?"

"Please don't play games with me. If you're going to kill me, just get it over with."

Logan chuckled.

"Why would we kill you?"

"Your brothers' eyes are glowing, and they're watching me as if they're angry and hungry."

Logan held her with one arm and reached to her face with the other as he held her gaze but continued walking.

"They're hungry for your pussy, not to take your life."

Melissa felt her cunt immediately drip from Logan's words alone. She felt her cheeks heat, and that heat ran through her body.

"Oh," was her only response as they reached the front entrance to a large house.

* * * *

She couldn't see anything until they entered and turned on a light in what appeared to be a living room. She had the feeling that they did this out of courtesy for her. It was obvious that wolves had excellent night vision.

Logan paused by the stairs.

"Tonight you are ours to explore and ravish."

He carried her upstairs and down the hallway to a bedroom.

Again, it was dark, and she could hardly see anything around her.

Frankie turned on a small light near the doorway. It cast a gentle glow around the room, baring the men to her viewing.

* * * *

Logan placed Melissa down on her feet on the carpeting then kissed her softly on the lips. He cupped her breasts as he slowly released her lips and took a step back.

As Melissa opened her eyes, they widened in pure shock. His brothers had removed their clothing, and all five men stood in front of her completely naked.

She placed one hand over her pussy and attempted to cover both her breasts with one arm.

"It's a little late for modesty, Mel," Sunny teased, taking a step toward her.

She looked up at him with eyes filled with fear and anticipation before he pulled her to him.

* * * *

Sunny could hardly wait to taste his woman. The long walk across the yard had been as torturous as the decision of who would fuck their mate next. He won the draw along with Jake, who was now making his way behind Melissa.

"You have the perfect body, Mel. There's no need to hide it from us," Sunny whispered before kissing her deeply and taking her fully into his arms. His cock tapped against her belly indicating the significant height difference between himself and his mate. She was petite compared to them, but then again, they were giants. Standing at over six feet four inches, they towered over most men.

The way she accepted Logan proved she wasn't fragile, yet the feel of her soft skin and sight of her big brown eyes made him want to be gentle. But he was a hungry man and his wolf wanted its share as well. He held her neck and face with one hand then cupped her left breast in the other. He was amazed that it didn't fit as he tried to gather her breast in his one hand. He felt his cock jerk forward and hit Melissa's skin. She moaned and closed her eyes. Delicate and slow may not happen after all.

* * * *

Melissa felt herself giving into Sunny's embrace and control. The feel of his muscles and intensity of his stare brought on waves of sexual awareness. She absorbed his size. The man was huge, as were his brothers, but Sunny had a wild look about him. His shoulder-length hair, the firm, set chin appeared chiseled and defined, all indicated his masculinity and sex appeal. This close proximity aroused her senses. Every erogenous zone in her body was aware of the length and hardness of his cock as it pressed against her stomach and made her desire more of him, them. His firm hold on her breast caused tiny vibrations to run through her body. His hand was enormous, and the feel of his strong, calloused fingers brushing against her nipple made her lose her breath. She gasped when she felt another set of hands on her shoulders and another cock press against her spine.

"Oh, God," she moaned softly, closing her eyes and swaying between them.

Jake massaged her shoulders. His firm hands attempted to loosen her tense muscles. It was a lost cause with Sunny's tongue exploring her mouth at the same time. Her insides coiled up as tight as a spring. Sunny released her lips, pulling the bottom lip between his teeth before gently releasing them. She was about to combust, and there wasn't even a cock pressed in any orifice of her body yet. Sunny kissed down her neck to her breasts.

Her nipples tingled as he nibbled and sucked on her right breast and attempted to get as much of her breast as he could into his mouth.

Her left breast burned with desire for his touch, but Jake took that moment to reach one hand over her rib cage and cup her breast with his hand. Jake massaged, pulled, and pinched her nipple, making her pussy drip. The sight of her own breast tilted forward with the nipple pink and hard made her belly muscles tighten. Their touch alone was taking her to near orgasm. A small amount of fluid dripped from her mound.

They inhaled together then released low growls against her skin that caused tiny goose bumps to scatter over her flesh. She squeezed her thighs together begging for strength to not weaken and cum. Her lack of experience was showing.

"I smell your desire for us. I can't wait to latch on to that delicate, wet, pink pussy of yours and get my fill," Sunny whispered as his warm breath collided against her skin.

Sunny caressed her inner thigh and slowly lifted it up and over his bulky shoulder. She felt his muscles on the delicate skin under her knees and nearly went weak.

Jake balanced her, taking over the job of thoroughly arousing her breasts just as Sunny pressed a finger to her cunt.

Her sharp intake of breath was heard through the silence in the room. She thrust forward and back between Sunny's thick finger and Jake's hard body.

"That's right, Mel. You feel the heat, the need for us to be inside of you," Jake whispered in her ear. His warm breath smacked against her skin, causing a tingling sensation to harden her nipples. Jake licked her ear lobe and nibbled, causing goose bumps to scatter across her neck and shoulders.

Sunny added a second digit, then finger-fucked her while she tried to remain upright. Just as she felt herself begin to lose the battle and explode, he pulled his fingers from her body.

She gasped in annoyance. "Please," she begged. Her body needed to feel their touch. She craved their attack now, no longer wanted to fight it.

"You like how that feels, Mel?' Sunny asked as he gently pressed his thumb to her oversensitive flesh.

"You're so nice and wet. She's glistening, and it's so beautiful," Sunny whispered. Between his warm breath colliding with her feminine folds and his deep stare at her pussy Melissa moaned.

He leaned forward and blew warm breath against her as he spread her pussy lips. She panted and tilted her hips toward his mouth, begging to be touched, licked, fucked, or anything. Then she felt his tongue lash out against her folds. She moaned again. He took that moment to lick every inch of her pussy while she lay there helpless and hanging by a thread. Jake covered her mouth with his own and kissed her breathless. Her chest pushed forward as Sunny replaced his tongue with two fingers and pushed them into her deep. She pulled her mouth from Jake's kiss to catch her breath.

Her legs began to wobble as if they would give out at any moment. His knuckles tapped firmly against her pubic bone as his fingers caused more of her cream to flow.

Then she felt Sunny's tongue against her pussy lips, spreading them and thoroughly tasting her cream-covered flesh again. She didn't think she could take any more.

Her knees gave out, but strong arms caught her. Jake. He was built as solid as a tree trunk. Thick yet trim, she could feel his muscles against her back. The man didn't have an ounce of fat on him.

"Whoa, baby, I've got you," he whispered as Sunny devoured her. His long, thick tongue pushed in and out of her pussy. It felt as if it grew longer and thicker with every stroke. Was it his wolf's tongue? The thought didn't scare her. It intensified the need for more of him.

"Please, Sunny, more," she begged, and he pulled his tongue from her, leaving her gasping for air.

In an instant, Sunny set her leg down, and Jake turned her around to face him.

What did she do? What did she say that made them stop?

"Sunny?" she whispered, about to ask him what happened when Jake turned her toward the bed.

There was Sunny sprawled out with his cock in his fist, his legs wide open, and his wild, shoulder-length brown hair pressed against the light beige comforter. Rippling muscles and a twinkle in his eyes, she felt herself blush. Her mouth watered at the sight of him.

Before she could make a move, Jake lifted her up and placed her on top of Sunny. Again, it took no effort for any of them to lift her.

She held Sunny's gaze, and the wild look in his eyes sent trepidation through to her core. He appeared untamable, just like his brother Logan. They shared the shoulder-length hair, the intense stare, and an intimidating demeanor. Their husky, firm bodies intimidated her. As if sensing her reservations, Jake caressed her shoulders from behind while he cupped her breasts by reaching under her arms.

She moaned against him, raising her hips in the air, giving Sunny room to arrange her to his liking.

"That's it, Mel. Don't be afraid. He won't break you," Jake teased and nibbled on her earlobe.

The chills ran though her skin at Jake's words. Her desire to feel their cocks inside her heightened to an almost desperate level.

She watched as Sunny slid his thick, long fingers up and down his shaft.

"Ride me, baby. I want you to fuck me and milk my cock with that tight, wet pussy of yours."

Melissa felt her insides tighten right before she spilled liquid from her pussy.

"Oh, yeah, baby. You're coming like you've sprung a leak and I haven't even got my cock in you yet." Sunny chuckled.

Jake lifted her hips and helped her align her cunt with Sunny's cock. As he trailed a finger over her back entrance, she shivered with trepidation.

Jake's hands tightened on her waist as he slowly lowered her inch by inch over Sunny. Melissa groaned at the wonderful fullness of the steely thickness. Facing Sunny, she saw his distorted expression as if he were in pain. She realized as she lowered more, that Sunny wasn't even halfway inside of her yet. She grabbed Jake's wrists and froze in place. "You're okay, Mel. You're doing just fine." Jake licked and nibbled on her spine. When he bit into her shoulders and tongued her skin, she felt herself relaxing as moisture lubricated her vagina and allowed Sunny's girth to fill her. Sunny moaned and grabbed her hips just as Jake released them. She felt Jake lick down her spine to the crevice between her ass cheeks again. Every time he did that, she was filled with mixed emotions. She had never had anal sex before and never considered it. But it seemed inevitable while bedding five men. She swallowed hard and hoped she could handle this. Sunny pushed up, making his cock push further inside of her cunt .

She grunted along with Sunny and finally pulled him most of the way inside.

When Sunny grabbed her breasts, cupped them with his enormous hands, and thrust up into her, she nearly flew off of him. Straddling him, her legs hardly reached the mattress. He was so big. But the more her pussy squeezed his cock, the more it wanted.

"That's it, Melissa. Just like that, fuck him good," Jake cheered her on, and something carnal came over her. She wanted to be in control. She wanted to fuck him as good as she would get fucked.

Up and down, she found her rhythm. She spread her legs wider and watched Sunny clench his teeth and pull on her nipples. She moaned and grunted. She lifted her rear, placed her feet flat on the comforter alongside his thighs, and squatted up and down, fast and hard until she was near exhaustion. It was like at the club as she danced and knew they were watching her. They had been turned on just as she was. Her thighs burned and her pussy wept, but Sunny felt so incredible and so damn hard, she didn't want to stop.

The multiple sounds of growls filled the room. To the right, Vince and Jake held their cocks in their fists and waited for their turn.

She looked at Sunny and his determined expression. Something was going on, but she wasn't sure what. She got her answer as she felt Jake slap her ass cheek. The sudden sting nearly halted her rhythm., The second smack landed on her other ass cheek and nearly did her in.

"You've been a naughty girl, Melissa. We like naughty," Jake stated. He rubbed a finger from her wet pussy to her forbidden hole.

She immediately stopped and tried to turn toward him.

"Please don't."

Sunny shook her hips, making her look at him and fall forward against his chest. She swung her head back to get her hair out of the way. At some point the ponytail holder must have broken.

Sunny held her chin in a firm grip.

"You've never been fucked in the ass, Mel?"

She shook her head and swallowed hard.

"We'll be your first and your only," Jake stated from behind her while he massaged her shoulders and her back.

"I don't know," she began to say until Sunny covered her mouth with his own. He kissed her passionately, making her relax into his hold as he thrust slowly up into her.

Jake was behind her, rubbing, caressing, and licking every inch of her. Slowly, she lifted up to meet Sunny thrust for thrust as her insides tightened. She was almost there and felt the pull for more. At that moment she sensed Jake's finger trail over her crevice. Then she felt the palm of his other hand over her hip.

She continued to thrust onto Sunny's cock, milking him for more in hopes that he could ease her need. Jake pressed his finger over the puckered hole. "Oh, oh that feels so good."

"It will feel real good, Mel. Will you let me make you feel good?" Jake whispered against her neck while he applied just a bit of pressure to her tight button but didn't penetrate it. God, she wanted to try it. She wanted to feel more of the erotic and naughty sensation.

"Yes, oh God, yes!"

Jake pressed his finger into her anus, and she felt a burning sensation, then a tingling.

Her body rocked from cock to digit as her cunt drenched Sunny's crotch.

"That's it, baby. Just like that, nice and easy. How does that feel, Mel? Feels good, right?" Jake asked, sounding breathless as he continued to press in and out of her hole. He added a second finger as she moaned.

"Yes."

"You want more, Mel? How about Jake's long, hard cock in your ass? It would feel so good. You belong to us now, Mel. We're never gonna let you go," Sunny chanted.

She was caught in the moment, in the sensation of it all. She wanted to believe that this was more than just incredible sex with five men. But people lied. Everyone had a scam or ulterior motives. Were the brothers an exception? She wasn't certain. All she knew was that they made her feel so good. They made her want them in every way.

"How about it, baby? I won't hurt you," Jake whispered while he continued to push inside of her.

She raised her ass and pushed back, giving him her answer.

He pulled his finger from her anus, and she felt her insides tighten with anticipation.

She felt the head of his cock at her entrance as Sunny thrust up into her repeatedly. She lost focus for a second, and that's when Jake pushed slowly through the tight rings.

"That's it, sweetheart. Just like that, let me into your sexy ass."

* * * *

"She's real tight, Jake. Take your fucking time with her. She's not some whore," Sunny threatened.

"I know that. You think I fucking don't know that? I would never hurt Mel. She's my mate, and this bonding process is important. She's too scared to trust anyone," Jake replied through their link.

"That's it, Mel. Just relax and enjoy this. Let Jake and I make love to you. You're so tight, Mel. You're so perfect," Sunny stated, pulling her down closer so he could kiss her lips again. He licked and explored her mouth, adding to the erotic sensations.

* * * *

"Oh. I'm so full!" Melissa felt the tightness inside her threaten to snap. The more they thrust their enormous cocks into her, the closer she came to snapping. Then she heard them both growl as they simultaneously pushed inside her. With Sunny's cock in her pussy and Jake's cock in her ass, she lost her breath.

Melissa moaned as the orgasm overtook her and she landed against Sunny's chest. Jake landed on top of her as all three of them panted for air.

* * * *

They waited a few moments, trying to decipher what the hell just happened.

"Did you feel that?" Jake asked Sunny.

"Fuck yeah! It was like nothing I've ever felt before," Jake replied.

"Heaven, man. Inside her is like heaven," Sunny added, and Jake agreed.

Jake slowly lifted up, pulling from Melissa's perfect body. He rubbed the palms of his hands over the globes of her ass, loving the look and feel of it. Glancing down at her and noticing her calm breathing, he wondered if she passed out. He gave a smack to her ass, and she jolted up.

"Hey!" Melissa exclaimed.

Sunny pulled her further up his chest as he pulled his cock from her pussy. He caressed her cheeks. "Hey, yourself." Then he kissed her.

* * * *

Melissa felt the bed dip and knew that Jake got up and left them. She felt odd for a moment. It was as if she missed him being so near. *What the hell is wrong with me?* She needed to get a grip. Just then the bed dipped again, and before she could lock gazes with Vince, he was pulling her off of Sunny and into his own arms. One glance at Sunny and he smiled then nodded toward Vince as if giving his approval for her to go to Vince.

"You're so beautiful, Mel," Vince stated as he ran his fingers through her hair before cupping her head and bringing her lips closer to his mouth. She felt his calmness and compassion. He was careful as he rolled her to her side then pressed his thigh between her legs. Cupping her face between his hands, he stared into her eyes.

"Everything is going to be just fine now, Mel. You'll be safe with us. Always," he whispered, then kissed her chin, her neck, and shoulder. Vince cupped her breast and stared at the abundant flesh before leaning over it with his mouth and licking the nipple.

Melissa closed her eyes and moaned from the sensations. It appeared as if Vince was her delicate lover. He wanted to take things slowly and explore her body.

Vince made his way to her other breast, then pressed her legs apart so he could feast on her pussy. Slowly, and while looking up to hold her gaze, he licked her belly ring then the top of her mound.

"You're wet for me already, Mel."

Swiftly he climbed between her legs, pressed his chest to the comforter, then used his fingers to part her pussy lips. He stared at her flesh, and she felt embarrassed. She attempted to close her legs but received a sound of disapproval from Vince as he clicked his tongue at her.

Melissa felt her body lose control and orgasm from Vince's seduction. How could she continue to come like this and just from their explicit words and simple touch? What type of power or magic did they possess to do this to her? Did it have something to do with them being wolves? Why weren't they taken? How could men like these be single? There had to be something wrong with them aside from being able to turn into wolves.

Vince continued to play with her folds, and then he pressed a finger to her moistened cunt. She felt every sensation as he pushed the thick digit slowly up into her and then slowly pulled it out.

"Nice and yummy," he teased, licking the cream from his finger.

Melissa moaned as she tried to hold his head, but he was just out of reach.

"I've got something for you, baby," Frankie whispered as he joined them on the bed.

Her heart hammered in her chest. Frankie had a lethal kiss on him and looked to be the friskiest of the five.

She knew what he wanted as he fisted his thick cock in his hand and inched his way closer to her mouth. It was just like in her shower fantasy. She saw the pre-cum drip slowly from the mushroom top, and she wanted to taste him. Licking her lips caused numerous moans to erupt around her. Vince took that moment to add a digit to her pussy.

She moaned again, and Frankie pressed his cock between her lips. Melissa took him as deep as she could. She had only given head once, and it had been to avoid having sex. She lied to some guy she had gone on a date with and said she had her monthly friend. He was all pissed off after paying for dinner and acting like a gentleman all night. He had been a big guy. Not quite as big as these guys were, but still big enough for her to fear his wrath. She gave him the blow job so she could get home safely.

Trying to ignore the bad memory, she attempted to focus on Frankie. He had short brown hair, thick build just like Vince and Jake, he was sexy as damn hell.

But still the bad memory had her not really focusing.

Frankie cupped her cheek as he pulled his cock from her mouth. "Baby, what's wrong?"

"I'm sorry. Let me try again." She exhaled and felt Vince crawl up her body.

He kissed her belly then ran his hand across her waist. He squeezed her tight, and she felt his sincerity as he, too, asked her what was wrong.

She wondered if they really cared. Then she wondered why she was getting so caught up in connecting with them. She should just give them what they wanted and what she wanted. Sex. Hot, wild, passionate group sex.

But then she locked gazes with Vince. His warm smile, the look of passion and concern in his brown eyes made her lose perspective. This wasn't love. They weren't her boyfriends. They were a group of guys who liked to share one woman together. It had to be some sort of wolf thing. Plus, they wanted answers to questions they had yet to ask but eventually would. If and when they found out about her illegal pastime, their views of her would change.

She attempted to pull her legs up and wrap her arms around herself, but Vince stopped her. He pulled her against his chest and rolled to his back. Her breasts collided with his chest as his hand pressed against her ass cheek. Then she felt Frankie press his body against her side and brush her hair out of her face. They cuddled against her, trying to break her defenses down.

* * * *

"Something happened to her. She just had some sort of bad memory and froze up or something," Vince stated through their link.

"Do you think someone forced himself on her?" Frankie asked, sounding upset that he made her suck his cock. Maybe she didn't like that or maybe someone made her do it.

"Don't jump to conclusions, and don't allow her to manipulate you. We don't know what Melissa is capable of," Logan interrupted.

* * * *

The silence was killing her. She actually missed their voices, their demands, as well as their hands and mouths touching her.

With a shaky breath and her ear and head pressed against Vince's chest, she spoke her mind.

"I'm sorry I couldn't." She paused as Frankie leaned over her, kissed her shoulder then palmed her breast.

"You're scared, and you don't quite understand what's going on between us," Frankie whispered.

She exhaled, and Vince took that moment to lift her up and make her straddle his hips. She sat up straight and held her palms against his muscular chest. Her breasts bobbed in the air at the sudden jolt, but she remained upright. Suddenly she felt a warm, tingly feeling inside of her. It was that same feeling that seemed to come and go when she was close to these men.

"Do you feel that, Melissa?" Vince asked.

She inhaled then exhaled. "Feel what?" Her response sounded lame to her own ears.

"That warm, tingly feeling that is covering your body. It's running through your veins and straight to your pussy," he whispered then thrust up against her ass and cunt. His words, his description were right on the mark. Her pussy dripped, and she closed her eyes.

"It's the mating musk. It's our wolves sending out a message to your body and soul, telling you that you belong to us. Feel it, Melissa, and embrace it," he concluded as he thrust up against her again.

Mel felt herself lose control and a hunger build up inside of her. She lifted her ass and lined Vince's cock with her entrance.

"Show me how good it feels, Mel. Let me hear you moan and cry for more of our cocks."

She slowly pressed down, taking Vince's thick cock deeper into her cunt, but he had different plans as he rammed up and into her. Melissa moaned a soft scream at the sudden invasion. Her body rocked up and down with Vince's until finally she caught a rhythm and rode him well.

Vince's brown eyes sparkled then glowed as she rocked her hips and locked gazes with him. Her pussy ached and craved more of him. It wasn't enough, and suddenly she felt as if she were starving for cock.

At that very moment she felt Frankie move in behind her and wipe his finger from her pussy to her back entrance. He pressed her back down so she was forced against Vince's chest. Vince pinched her nipple then pulled her against him, covering her mouth in a voracious kiss. It was hot and wild, and just as she caught herself battling for control, Frankie's hard, long cock pressed through her back entrance and through the tight rings making her scream her release.

They moved in sequence, one after the next. In and out, up and down, the bed creaked and moaned from their fucking fest. Every single part of her tingled and burned. Frankie grabbed a handful of her hair, pulling her back against him as he quickly sucked her mouth, released it then sucked her neck, biting the skin. Their hips thrust at the same time, and her breasts bobbed in the air while Vince grabbed at them. It was out of control and so erotic she thought she would die from the pleasure.

With one arm she held Vince against his shoulder and chest, and her other arm reached back to Frankie's backside as she grabbed his ass. It was sensational.

Frankie increased his speed then shoved deep into her cunt, chanting her name. "Fuck, Melissa!"

He shot his essence into her anus as Vince continued to thrust up into her.

Frankie pulled out of her, making her gasp, but then Vince rolled her to her back, lifted her legs over his shoulders, and thrust into her harder. It was wild and sexy, the way he took control and seemed to need more of her. She panted for air and absorbed every sensation. She knew a situation like this would never happen again.

His balls slapped against her ass as he thrust his cock deep into her cunt at record speed. The sound of the headboard hitting the wall added to the erotic encounter. She caught herself losing focus, but she held on to his head and shoulders, scratching and grabbing what she could.

Vince increased his speed then growled as his hips thrust deeper, penetrating her better and causing her to orgasm. She screamed as the shakes filled her body and dizziness overtook her.

"Mine," Vince growled as he leaned forward and bit her shoulder just as he exploded inside of her.

Melissa's last conscious thoughts were of Vince's tongue licking her shoulder then the sound of growls filling the room.

* * * *

Vince stared at Melissa as she slept in the bed. Frankie and Sunny lay on either side of her.

"I can't believe I bit her," he whispered as he twirled one of the chocolate locks around his finger then released it.

"It wasn't your fault, Vince, and it was going to happen eventually, anyway," Frankie replied.

"Sometimes the wolf knows better than the man," Sunny added.

"But we should have marked her together," Vince added, feeling guilty.

"It doesn't matter. We all fucked her and loaded her body up with our seed. She's ours, and that's the bottom line. Biting her sends a message to other wolves that she is ours," Logan stated firmly from across the room.

"Let's get some rest. We have a lot to discuss with our little dancer in the morning," Sunny replied.

"It is morning," Jake added sarcastically as he yawned then curled up on the bottom of the bed. He wanted to remain as close as possible to his mate.

* * * *

Melissa awoke to the sound of her cell phone ringing. She heard the mumbled ring and knew it remained in her purse from last night. The men must have brought it inside. She felt the two heavy bodies next to her. Frankie had a hand over her breast, and Sunny had his hand over her pussy. Unbelievable. These men seemed to have voracious appetites when it came to the female body. She slowly began to remove their hands and crawl from the bed. She crawled in between Frankie's big legs and Jake's head then off the bed. A quick glance into the corner of the room and she noticed Vince and Logan were present as well. They were all in the same room together all night.

She grabbed her bag and answered the phone just in time.

"Hello," she whispered.

"Sorry, Mel, I started to get worried when I didn't hear back from you this morning. Where are you?"

"I'm kind of busy right now."

"Wait, I took care of everything the way you told me."

"Good. We'll talk about it later, not now."

"But the banker tried to take the money from me, and then he tried to attack me."

Melissa felt her insides heat up inside.

"That piece of crap! Did he hurt you, Celine?"

"No. Thank god the guard was nearby. He heard the whole conversation and called the manager."

"Geez, Celine, you were lucky. I wish you would have waited for me."

"Then what? You would have probably decked the guy and wound up in jail. Not after everything you did last night. You saved our lives, Melissa. My babies would have wound up in foster care somewhere, and I would have wound up in jail or dead. I owe you my life."

"You know I would never let that happen to you guys."

"I know, your aunt told me about the foster care when you were a kid and about some of the rough times. You're the best, Mel. This neighborhood and I owe you so much."

"Quit it now, Celine. It was nothing. How are my babies?" Mel asked as she pulled a blanket from the bed and cuddled up in a ball on the rug against the bottom of the bed.

"They're fine, and they miss you. When are you coming home?"

"Soon. Probably later today. Aunt Peggy has that checkup this afternoon. I really need to get going. This isn't a good time right now."

"Don't worry. I'll take her. Besides, you need a little rest. Wherever you are and whoever you're with, enjoy it for a little bit. You deserve it."

Melissa was taken aback. "What makes you think I'm with someone?"

"I have kept you on the phone for more than a minute and you haven't hung up on me yet. Usually you're on your way to the next responsibility or next job. Oh shit! I forgot to tell you that Jamie Montgomery stopped by to see you. I didn't know you knew Jamie so well."

"Who said I did?"

"He kind of hinted at it. He said something about dinner and that he needed to speak to you."

Melissa swallowed hard. Detective Jamie Montgomery wanted her help, but she wasn't taking the bait.

"Oh, well, I'll call him later."

"See you in a little while, Mel."

Melissa closed her cell phone and leaned back against the bottom of the bed and the floor.

She had been living in a fantasy. She had forgotten about her responsibilities and had been selfish. She needed to leave. She should be home caring for Aunt Peggy, dealing with Celine's problems, and focusing on the kids.

But instead, she began to feel the men around her, actually feel them inside her heart and her soul. What did they do to her last night? What type of spell or secret powers did these men have besides the ability to shift? More importantly, what did they want from her?

She slowly rose from the floor and looked around her. All five men lay sleeping. A glance past the bed and she knew that there was a bathroom, perhaps even a shower she could use while they remained sleeping. But then she looked toward the other door and contemplated escape. She wasn't going to get very far naked.

She tiptoed to the bathroom and closed the door.

* * * *

"What do you think?" Sunny asked Logan.

"She's not going to stick around long," Logan replied.

"What about Jamie Montgomery going to see her? I don't like it," Frankie added.

"Maybe he's interested in our little dancer," Jake added to the conversation.

"Then we should let him know that she's ours," Vince replied.

"We wait and see. I'm still not certain I believe her story about why she was at the warehouse last night." Sunny added.

"I agree. She needs a more thorough interrogation," Frankie replied.

"We'll work on her and see what we can find out," Logan stated, then rose from the chair and walked to the bathroom.

* * * *

Melissa heard the door open to the first small room attached to the shower room. There were double sinks and a small changing area. After opening up a few cabinets she found the towels. Then through another set of doors were a separate shower and a separate bathtub. Both were to die for. She had been tempted to take a bath, but that would have been presumptuous. This whole situation was confusing, and she was completely flying by the seat of her pants. She needed to get out of here. She ignored the sounds and focused on the hot water as it massaged her sore muscles. Some body parts ached from all the stress, and others ached from overuse after being unused for so long. She giggled at the thought. She never thought she would feel sore and content after sex. She was content, yet she craved more of them. Melissa tried to convince herself that it was a natural response to such charismatic and handsome men. Most women would die to be where she had been last night and early this morning. Who knew how many women the crew took home and had their way with daily like this. Any minute they would kick her out. She waited for their words of dismissal. "Time to leave, Melissa. Thanks for the free sex. We'll call you sometime." She felt the ache. Did she really think that their passion and their attentiveness during sex meant they wanted a relationship? Foolish her. Then Vince even bit her. What was that all about? Was it their mark to keep track of the women they fucked? What happened to little black books or private files on their BlackBerrys?

She placed her hands on the tile wall and let the water caress her shoulders as she hung her head. She couldn't fight the disappointed feeling of being used. Why didn't she fight them off? Like she would have had a chance.

* * * *

Logan watched Melissa as she pressed her palms against the shower wall and let the water hit her voluptuous body. He could see how tense she was, but his focus was on her beauty. He admired the toned muscles in her arms as they flexed against the wall accompanied by toned shoulders and a firm back and the way her ass curved out perfectly. Even the cheeks of her ass had the best little curve to them as they met her long, thin thighs. She was perfection, and he couldn't stay away.

When he approached her, he pressed the palms of his hands above hers on the wall, letting his torso and cock softly touch her ass and back. She didn't stir or act surprised by his presence. She had sensed him way before he entered the shower.

Logan kissed her neck where Vince had bitten her. She let out a small gasp, and then he rubbed his erect cock against the crevice of her ass as he slowly pumped against her.

Reaching one hand down the wall and under her arm to her breast, he found her nipple hard and aroused, and then he pulled gently on it.

"I missed you, Melissa." He inhaled her scent and wrapped his arm around her waist. "You smell so good. Did you miss me, too?" he asked.

"Yes."

Logan used his leg to spread her legs then rubbed his hand from her breasts over her tight abs to her pussy. When he pressed a finger between her folds, she pushed her ass back and moaned.

"Are you wet for me, Melissa?"

She nodded her head, and he lifted his thigh, raising her ass as he bent his knees.

He fisted his cock in one hand and held Melissa around the waist with his arm as he pressed his cock near her pussy from behind. He pretended that he couldn't find her cunt, and when Melissa took his cock in her hand and pressed it to her entrance, he knew she craved it, too.

Slowly, he pushed forward, and she lifted her ass and bent closer to the tile wall so he could penetrate her fully.

In and out, with careful, deep thrusts, Logan made love to Melissa. He didn't fuck her, he didn't worry about giving it to her good, and he just focused on the feel of being inside and connected to his mate.

Her quiet moans of pleasure hardened his cock and brought him to near orgasm sooner than he was ready to allow.

He focused on her beauty.

He kissed her neck and palmed her breasts as he thrust up and into her.

"You feel tight and warm and perfect, Melissa." He meant those words, and he meant to tell her that he was never going to let her go. He realized that no matter what she had done or no matter how hard she tried to push him and his brothers away, that they would come back for her and get her.

He could feel her body tighten and the signs that she was about to orgasm, so he increased his thrusts. She kept her palms against the wall and it drove his beast mad with possessiveness and power. Whether she knew it or not, it was a show of submission to allow him to take her from behind as she kept her palms against the wall and her body open to him. The way she looked, the way his cock felt, buried deep inside her as the water showered between them and his balls hit her ass causing a sloshing sound to fill the shower, all embedded in his mind. He would remember this moment and their connection both physical and emotional. Harder and harder he increased his speed as his eyes focused on her neck and his brother's mark.

She moaned louder and louder until finally Logan thrust deeper, and together they exploded just as he bit into her shoulder next to Vince's mark. Melissa screamed, and Logan had to hold her up as the after-effects nearly overtook both of them.

* * * *

Melissa felt herself weaken in Logan's embrace. She was dazed at what just took place between them. At least she felt as if it meant something, but aside from him biting her, he didn't appear as affected as she was. He turned her toward him, and before she could get a good look into his eyes, he covered her mouth with his own. He kissed her thoroughly. She rubbed her hands all over every bit of him she could, from his shoulder-length hair, his muscular shoulders and neck to his sides, and his ass. It was like touching marble with a slight layer of human skin over it. When he finally released her lips, he rose up to full height, and she realized just how big he actually was. Her breasts lined up closer to his belly than his chest. As if sensing her sudden fear and reservations about their size difference, Logan lifted her up so that she straddled his hips as he held her against the tile.

Instinctively, she wrapped her arms around his neck and looked into his eyes. They were a deep chocolate brown and had bright green specks inside of them.

"You keep looking at me like that and we'll never make it to breakfast."

Breakfast? Come to think of it, she was feeling kind of hungry. But what would she wear?

"I don't have anything to wear," she whispered.

"Vince is taking care of that. Although I don't think you'll be needing anything to wear for the rest of the day."

She felt herself blush at his words. Then reality began to hit her.

"I can't stay, Logan. I have responsibilities."

He crinkled his eyebrows. "You'll stay until we release you."

"I can't, Logan. I have my kids to care for, and my aunt has an appointment."

"Celine is taking her, remember?" he shot back at her, and her heart hammered in her chest. He had heard her conversation with Celine before. Oh God, did Melissa give up any information during that phone call? Panic sunk in.

"You look a little guilty, Melissa." He slowly let her down and turned off the water in the shower. When they emerged, Frankie stood there, hair wet, fully dressed and holding a towel for her. He threw the other one at his brother but held her gaze. It didn't take a genius to know that they were upset with her.

Frankie pulled her into his arms and lifted her up to carry her to the bedroom.

* * * *

After thoroughly drying her body and her hair, Vince walked in carrying some clothes. He placed a green military tank top and a pair of boxers on the bed.

"We'll be downstairs waiting," Vince said, and they walked out of the bedroom.

Melissa let the towel fall off her body, and she stared at the boxers and tank. Pulling the tank top on, she realized it was more like a muscle tee than a regular tank top. Her breasts were large, and this was a new tank right out of the bag. But it was still one of the men's. The tank reached her knees and looked more like a tank dress than a top on her. The boxers were way too big, so she opted to wear just the tank. They had seen her in less, anyway. She took a deep breath and slowly walked out of the bedroom and down the stairs.

* * * *

They waited in the kitchen. Jake cooked a bunch of food, and the rest helped put out plates, forks, napkins, and glasses for drinks. They were extremely hungry, and wolves needed lots of nourishment, especially after sex.

They all stopped what they were doing the moment they heard Melissa approach.

Jake felt his mouth drop at the sight of her. Through their link, his brothers added numerous comments about how sexy Mel looked. Their woman was a knockout. She even made an ugly military-green tank top look sexy. Her abundant breasts appeared as if they would pour out of the sides of the top. Her shoulders and arms looked toned and sexy. She clasped her hands in front of her and placed her hair behind one ear as she avoided their gazes. She looked shy and innocent, as if their stares embarrassed her.

The tank top was baggy in front of her and just reached about an inch above her knee.

It was Frankie who walked over to her first.

"Damn, dancer, I've never seen anyone look as good as you do in that tank top."

"It's kind of big," she whispered as he took her hand and slowly turned her around.

"No boxers, huh?" he teased then caressed the material over her backside.

"They were way too big."

"This will do just fine," Frankie whispered, pulling her into his arms and kissing her. She felt nearly breathless by the time he released her. That same hunger began to build up inside of her. When Frankie released her lips, she felt another set of hands on her hips. Jake. She knew it was him, but as he leaned his face over her shoulder and inhaled against her neck, she felt relieved. It was odd. They had only left her alone for ten or fifteen minutes, tops. How did she become so needy for their touch?

"You smell real good, Mel," Jake whispered as his kissed her neck and rubbed his cock against her ass. Immediately, her nipples hardened to tiny pebbles, and the hunger grew.

It was Sunny who walked in front of her next. He placed his hands on her hips then caressed her body, being sure to cup her breasts and tease her already too-sensitive nipples. She closed her eyes and exhaled as her insides coiled up tighter. Jake pulled away, and Vince took his place, catching her as she swayed from Sunny's touch. Sunny cupped her neck and head with his hand, leaned down, and kissed her thoroughly.

"Now that's the kind of 'good-morning kiss' I can get used to," he whispered before releasing her.

Melissa's heart hammered in her chest every time they mentioned any words or indication of this thing between them lasting or extending. They couldn't be serious.

Vince's arms wrapped around her waist, enveloping her body in muscle. It was a good thing that she loved a man with muscles because these men had them everywhere.

"Where's my good-morning kiss, Mel?" Vince asked as he inhaled her scent against her neck and hair. She was starting to get used to men sniffing her and touching her constantly and the way they inhaled her scent and responded to her body's reaction to their touch. She felt the moisture leak from her pussy.

Vince turned her body around so she faced him. He locked gazes with her, and she saw his desire. He smiled softly then kissed her lips as he rubbed his hands over her ass.

Melissa heard someone clear their throat, but she wasn't sure who it was.

"Time for breakfast," Logan stated firmly, and Vince released her lips then took her hand. She thought he would lead her to the empty chair next to Jake, but instead, he walked her over to Logan and the empty seat between him and Sunny.

Even while sitting, Logan towered over her.

Vince stood her in front of Logan then walked away leaving her standing in front of Logan helpless. Her heart beat rapidly as she locked gazes with a very intimidating and fierce-looking man. His shoulder-length hair was shiny and beautiful. She had the urge to run her fingers through it, but it appeared that Logan was in charge. A move like that could cost her. Instead, she stared right back at him, waiting for him to speak.

She kept her distance until finally he spoke.

"Where's my good-morning kiss?" he asked in such a demanding and superior tone she felt conflicted. Part of her wanted to give him more than just a good-morning kiss, and part of her wanted to challenge him.

Slowly she walked closer to him. Unlike the others Logan didn't reach for her or pull her into his arms and kiss her. He wanted her to show the affection, the desire, and surprisingly, Melissa had no problem with that.

His legs were open as he sat on the stool. She walked between them and slowly reached her hands out to place her palms against his waist. She rubbed along his ribs then his chest, holding his gaze. His nostrils flared as he looked her over from cleavage to neck.

Melissa looked down and saw the rung under the stool. She stepped up on it, climbing between his legs as she ran her fingers through his chocolate locks. She felt her heavy breathing. She felt the need to taste Logan and the desperate need for his touch.

She leaned closer. She held his gaze then kissed his chin, his neck, and then his cheek before finally reaching his strong, determined lips. He was a superior man. Melissa acknowledged that with every ounce of her soul. All the Valdamar brothers were superior, strong, and perhaps invincible. As she kissed him, she waited for his touch and to feel his hands around her waist. The anticipation overtook her actions. She climbed higher onto his lap. She kneeled on his rock-solid thighs as she held his hair, tugging it and pulling it while she kissed him thoroughly.

Finally his hands touched her thighs then slowly moved under the material of the tank top to her ass cheeks. All the brothers had such large hands and thick fingers. They knew how to arouse a woman. They had her pegged immediately and knew just how to touch her. He squeezed her ass cheeks, and she moaned into his mouth. Without thinking, she began to thrust her hips against him.

That's when she felt his fingers against the crevice of her ass caressing the too-sensitive pathway to her pussy. Logan pressed a thick digit into her cunt, and she gasped from the impact, her body oversensitive after all the men thoroughly kissed her and touched her this morning. It had been too much.

"Fuck yeah, Mel," Frankie stated from across the table.

Logan pulled his mouth from Melissa's, lifted her up by her hips, and placed her right on the island next to the food. She gasped from his abrupt move and panted as she saw his eyes glowing like never before. The sound of plates moving and the men doing things behind her weren't important to her. She wanted to know what Logan planned on doing to her next.

* * * *

Logan's wolf couldn't take it any longer. He needed to claim his mate. Without hesitation, he pulled Melissa's legs forward so her pussy lined up over the edge of the table where he could feast on her. Sunny caught her as she fell backwards so she wouldn't hit the table.

He gave his brother a silent nod then set his eyes on Melissa's glistening cunt.

"Change of plans, baby. I'm having you for breakfast," he told her firmly, and Melissa moaned as Logan plunged his tongue between her pussy lips. His wolf was gaining control fast. If he didn't fuck and claim her, he might shift. It was so unbearable.

As he ate her cream, he felt his tongue elongate and Melissa shake her head side to side and thrust her hips forward.

"You're so hot, Mel. Damn, I could come in my pants just watching you," Jake stated as he leaned over and licked her lips then covered her mouth in a voracious kiss.

Logan took the opportunity to unzip his pants and free his engorged cock from confinement. He felt about to burst, so he pulled Melissa closer to the edge of the table, lined up his cock to her pussy, and shoved forward, making her scream.

"Yes!" Melissa roared.

Logan felt out of control. He didn't want to hurt her, but he felt the fight between the man and the beast.

He sensed his eyes changing and slowed his pace as he ground his teeth, trying not to shift inside of Mel.

Then he heard her gentle voice.

"It feels so good, Logan."

"I don't want to hurt you." He bit out his words, and she looked scared, but she still tried to calm him. She was amazing. Despite not knowing anything about shifters or being their mate, she remained strong and confident as she tried to console him. Him of all people?

"You won't, Logan. Now let yourself go. I need to feel you deep inside of me. I don't why I feel this way or what in the world is happening to me, but I need you like this," she stated then thrust her hips forward.

Logan shoved back, sending his cock deeper, and then he lifted her thighs over his shoulders, causing only Melissa's shoulders to remain on the table as he plunged into her. Thrust after thrust she chanted him on. She begged him for more until finally they exploded together, and he growled against her shoulder as he bit her. His wolf slowly calmed down as it realized it marked her as his mate. He held her against him. They gasped for air then kissed one another.

Sunny cleared his throat, and when he opened his eyes, he saw the others watching them and smiling.

"Breakfast will never be the same on this table again," Vince teased, and they all chuckled.

Melissa glanced at her hair, the ripped tank top, and the way her naked body was displayed on their kitchen table. A blush covered her chest, and Logan laughed.

"You're going to have to lose that modesty of yours, Mel," Frankie teased as Logan helped her sit up then pulled her into his arms.

"I think I have egg in my hair," she stated.

"Let me see," Jake replied, sounding ready to help. Then he leaned in to sniff her, tickling her neck and making her laugh.

There had to be a way to work this situation out. They weren't going to give up their mate. Not without a fight.

* * * *

Melissa felt a bit embarrassed now that she was completely naked and the men were all dressed. Even Logan pulled his jeans back on.

"Maybe you can throw my clothes in the wash so I can wear them home," she suggested.

"You won't be going home for a while," Logan interrupted abruptly, and the others moved to sit. Frankie squeezed her hand and led her to an empty seat between Logan and Sunny. She hesitated, standing there until Logan gave her the evil eye. Immediately, she sat in the seat.

How could he be so compassionate and loving one second then completely bossy and obnoxious the next? And what did he mean she wasn't going home for a while? She had responsibilities.

The men began to eat, but she sat there, naked and annoyed.

"Okay. This is bullshit!" she stated as she rose from the chair.

"What?" Sunny asked her, but Logan just gave her the evil eye. She might have faltered at that stare the first dozen times, but not now. Now this was getting out of hand.

"I don't know what kind of kinky crazy shit you guys are into, but I am not sitting here naked while the rest of you are wearing clothes."

Sunny pulled off his T-shirt and tossed it at her.

"Wear this. It won't be on for long anyway," he stated confidently.

She pulled the shirt on, and of course it fell right past her knees.

Melissa placed her hands on her hips and stared at the five huge guys who continued to eat and half pay attention to her. She wasn't going to lose her cool. She had to think like them. She had to play them so she could get out of here. The longer she was around them, the more she fantasized about happy endings, princes on white horses, or in this case, wolves in men's clothing. Or whatever the saying was. Shit! They turned her mind to mush. She had shit to take care of and the kids.

"I need my clothes done. I need to get home to my kids and my aunt. Whether you believe me or not, they are my responsibility."

They were silent a moment, and then Sunny spoke.

"We know. They're your sister's kids. You took custody of them after her and her husband died in a drive-by shooting."

They had checked her out. They investigated her. How long have they been watching her? What else did they know?

"You look a little pale, Melissa. Sit down and eat something. We'll discuss this later," Logan stated, but she didn't want to eat. She felt sick to her stomach and dizzy with fear.

What was this all about? She had been trying so hard to help others and to take care of those she loved. What did these five men really want from her? Was it just sex? Was it some kind of secret game the police officers had, just like that secret club of Paul's?

The tears stung her eyes as she turned to walk away.

"Stop!" Vince commanded.

She didn't want to, but it was Vince. He had acted like he was sincere and empathetic to her emotions. He wasn't so demanding and bossy.

"Get over here now," he stated. *Oh, crap! What did I just say about Vince not being controlling and bossy?*

She knew that look and reluctantly gave in to his tone as well as the facial expressions of the soldiers around him.

When she approached, he lifted her up and placed her on his lap.

She swallowed hard. She could feel his muscular legs under her ass as well as his thick, hard cock. He wanted her.

Placing some eggs on a fork, he stared at her as he lifted it to her lips.

"Eat first. Then we'll talk."

She would have ignored his command, but then he gave that small, sexy smile of his, dimples and all. She gave in, and he continued to feed her.

Chapter 12

"She hasn't gone home yet. I left Deatrix there. He'll notify me as soon as she arrives," Chu told Bret.

"Where could she be? I mean, she has to return home soon to take care of those kids and that old aunt of hers. Are you sure she hasn't gone to see that new dealer?" Bret asked, sounding impatient to Chu.

"Yeah. He's been covered as well. I talked to Lester, too. He said someone in a black mask grabbed the bag of dough, but he also said that he didn't recognize the other guy he did the deal with. He said he was some tall Spanish guy. I sent Felix to investigate further. There may be another problem, though."

"What would that be? Considering I lost a hundred and fifty grand in drugs and money."

"Detective Jamie Montgomery."

"What the hell does he have to do with this?"

"He showed up at Mel's place looking for her. I also found out that Mel worked over at Paul's place Saturday night for a private party."

Bret banged his fist on the table.

"Fuck! You think she's a snitch for the cops?"

"Could be. I mean, when I think about all the shit you discussed on Friday night."

"You have to find her, and the second you do, you bring her to me."

"Yes, sir," Chu stated then left the room.

* * * *

Bret picked up the phone and made a call. "Hey, it's me, listen, I believe we have a problem," Bret told the other person on the line.

"What problem would that be?"

"Besides getting ripped off a shitload of fucking money, ah, let me think. Perhaps a voluptuous brunette we know fairly well. Seems she may have gotten herself involved with something that she's not quite cut out for. Have any ideas where I might find her?"

"No. The club is the best place to catch her. She's working tomorrow night, I know that much."

"Well, I appreciate the information. I'll call you when I'm ready for your services again," Bret stated.

"If it involves the brunette, I will definitely be waiting for the call."

The guy hung up before he could respond. Fuck! Melissa belonged to him. He wasn't going to kill her yet. He just needed to set her in her place by his side and in his bed.

He glanced at his watch. Twenty-four hours. He'd have her in his bed in less than twenty-four hours.

* * * *

Melissa sat on the couch in Sunny's T-shirt with her legs crossed and her hands clasped on her lap. Logan straddled a chair in front of her. Frankie sat sideways on her left and a few inches away while Vince sat on her right. His thighs rubbed up against her thighs, making it difficult to focus. Jake stood by the fireplace staring at her. It was Sunny who began to speak.

"We understand that you have responsibilities and kids to take care of, but you need to understand what's happening here between all of us. We're meant to be together."

She was silent a moment as she looked at the five men. They were truly a fantasy come true. But what did she have to offer them besides sex? She thought she felt something for them, but the one time she took a chance she had nearly died because of the decision. Bret could have owned her body, mind, and soul. Then there were her illegal activities to address. Sure, she got away with them, but if something else came up and money was needed, she would have a decision to make. These men could wind up being the ones who arrest her.

"Melissa, what are you thinking right now? Just talk to us and make us understand you," Vince suggested.

It was the hardest thing she ever had to do. She couldn't give in to their fantasy. These types of things don't happen in real life. The public doesn't accept ménage relationships. What about her kids and her aunt?

"I think you should get my clothes so I can leave."

"What?" Vince asked as he moved closer to her, taking her hand into his own.

She refused to look at him.

"I think I need to go home."

"You're thinking about the human's reaction and what people would say about you being with five men," Sunny stated.

"Of course I am, among other things," she replied.

"You mean the kids and your aunt? We'll make them understand," Jake added.

"Make them understand? I'm responsible for them. My brother in law and sister left me in charge of their lives, their future. These types of relationships are not the norm. How could we be affectionate and intimate with each other around them? It's just not feasible at this point in time," she stated then stood up from the couch.

"We can work it all out. If need be, we can leave New York and head closer to our packs. We get work all over the world, Melissa. We can handle this," Sunny added.

"I need to work to make money to support the family. What if my aunt has a relapse? I can't afford another ninety-thousand-dollar medical bill."

She looked at them with pleading eyes although all she wanted to do was run into their arms and be held. It was incredible and also surreal. She couldn't give in to the fantasy. "We can financially support you and your family. Any bills, expenses, even college for the kids later on in life, we can pay for," Logan stated.

"And in return, what? I stay in a relationship with five men and have sex at your beck and call? No true commitment. Just a contract between five men and one woman?"

"It's more than that," Frankie added.

"We're offering you a way out of past regrets and a financially secure future for you and your family. Isn't that what you're concerned about? Their well-being and their futures? We're promising to handle it all."

Melissa felt the pain in her chest at Logan's words.

Tears filled her eyes as she turned to him with a reply.

"I've never given my body or my soul for money, Logan. I sure as hell will not do it now."

She walked out of the room, leaving the men calling her name. She knew that Vince had washed and dried her clothes for her. She searched the bedroom and found them in the bathroom. She changed back into her uniform from Paul's. That's where the craziness had started.

Looking into the mirror, she saw the sadness in her eyes. She felt the feelings of guilt for her words against Logan. It was better this way. She needed to focus on the kids. She needed to help straighten out Celine's problem and get back to reality. It had been fun while it lasted, and she avoided jail one more time. Perhaps next time, if there was one, she wouldn't be so lucky.

Plus she had the rest of the money to hide. There were people who needed a little more help. She could take care of that and get the five most amazing men she ever met in her life out of her mind.

"I like Charlie's uniform more than this one."

Melissa jumped at the sound of Sunny's voice.

Melissa bent down to slip on the high heels. She wobbled a little, and Sunny grabbed her to help steady her. Her body collided with his massive one. He was a god in every aspect of the word. From his perfect looks to his muscular physique and incredibly intimidating demeanor, he had everything any woman would want. The fact that he was a man of the law added to his sex appeal, and knowing that he was a wolf and could shift at will made him untamable and a total risk. She just couldn't take the chance.

"I'm good," she whispered, and she was annoyed at how out of breath she sounded.

He remained holding her as he gently moved her long, brown hair out of her face while his other arm held her around her waist.

"I think you misunderstood what Logan meant downstairs."

She shook her head.

"I know what he meant, Sunny. I know what all of you mean. I can't take the chance you're asking me to take. I don't know any of you, and you don't know me."

He squeezed her tighter as he pressed her butt against the vanity. Holding her hips, giving them a squeeze that sent her body up in flames, he whispered.

"Get to know us. Let us show you who and what we are to you and what you are to us." He ran the palm of his hand along her curves, up over her breast to her neck, then leaned in to kiss her.

"We'll give you some time to think about it. Next time we come for you, be ready."

She felt the chills from his words as his lips covered hers. Sunny kissed her firmly and with meaning. So easily she could have given in to staying with him and his brothers. She warmed in his embrace. She visualized making love to them and being in their arms. If only what they had to offer was forever and for real. But it couldn't be. Everyone had an angle, a scam, and a plan to achieve their agenda. She wasn't going to be their agenda, and she wasn't going to risk her heart.

She began to pull away, and Sunny got the hint as he released her lips then pulled her against his chest.

"I'll drive you home."

* * * *

Melissa wasn't expecting Sunny to literally walk her to her door. She tried to make him leave, but he refused.

"I don't want the kids to get upset. I've never brought anyone home before. I don't do relationships, Sunny."

"And you'll never bring anyone home besides me or my brothers ever again," he stated firmly as he held her gaze. She began to respond when the door swung open and a multitude of kids ran into her hugging her.

"You're back! Yeah! Now we can start the party," Brandon began to say then froze in place.

Sunny's size was definitely intimidating. The kids looked concerned.

"Who is this?" Lea asked.

"Is this who you were with and why you didn't come home last night after work?" Brandon asked as Tommy practically climbed up Melissa's leg.

"This is my friend Sunny. He's a police officer," Melissa stated as she began to head inside the apartment. She felt kind of embarrassed about her small apartment and how many people squeezed into it, especially after seeing what kind of place Sunny and his brothers had. It was gorgeous.

"Let them in, kids, come on," Aunt Peggy called to them, and they all hurried through the door.

* * * *

"Do you play football?" Brandon asked Sunny as they walked further into the living room.

"I used to play in high school and a little in college."

"That's what I want to do. I want to play for the high school then go to Notre Dame and play ball. Aunt Mel said I could do whatever I set my heart on doing. I just have to study really hard and practice a lot."

Sunny smiled then glanced at Melissa. "Your aunt is right. Hard work pays off, and studying to get good grades is very important."

Sunny looked around at the small apartment and the amount of people who were there. There appeared to be only two bedrooms. There were three kids, Melissa, and her aunt. A pretty tight fit.

"This is my friend, Celine. Celine, this is Sunny."

"Hello, Sunny. It's nice to meet a friend of Mel's. She never brings anyone home. You must be special," Celine teased. He smiled at the attractive blonde. She seemed like she had a nice personality.

Melissa gave Celine a light punch in the arm.

"Actually, Sunny was just driving me off. He wanted to see me to the door to be sure I was safe," Melissa stated as if implying she wanted him to leave.

"Oh, can Sunny stay for dinner?" Brandon asked.

"Oh, I don't know what I'm making yet," Melissa stated.

"I took out the chicken cutlets you brought yesterday, and Deborah dropped off some homemade apple pie for dessert. She said that she wanted to thank you for getting the extra baby formula and money for the rent. You know, Melissa, I don't know how you keep up with helping everyone and saving money so you can take that last class and study for the bar exam."

"Aunt Peggy, please," Melissa interjected.

"She's an angel, our Melissa," Celine stated.

Melissa gave her a warning look.

"It's okay. I should really be going. I don't want to intrude," Sunny replied, but he really wanted to stay and get to know Melissa and her family. The kids were adorable. As he caught more of their scent, he could have sworn that he smelled wolf. But that couldn't be. Especially in the littlest one, Tommy. He clung to Melissa from the moment she got to the doorway.

"It's okay, Sunny. You're not intruding. We're actually leaving. I need to get ready for work tomorrow, and the kids need baths," Celine stated as she gathered up her three small children and everyone gave hugs and kisses good-bye.

Sunny absorbed it all. He felt the love they all shared.

"So, Sunny can stay for dinner?" Brandon asked.

"Sunny stay!" Tommy cheered as he began dancing around Sunny.

Melissa looked at Sunny with pleading eyes, but he couldn't resist.

"Chicken is one of my favorite meats," he teased as he looked deeply into Melissa's eyes. She immediately blushed then shook her head.

"Okay. Let me go change, and we can get started."

* * * *

When Melissa reentered the room, she felt the tears block her vision. Sunny was sitting with Lea and Brandon while Tommy sat on Sunny's lap playing with his hair. They were asking him questions about how he met their aunt and if he was her boyfriend.

"Hey, that's enough interrogating, you three. Let's get the table set and start preparing dinner for our guest," Melissa ordered with a smile.

* * * *

Everyone ran to the bathroom to wash their hands, then they all pitched in setting the table, taking out lettuce and tomatoes for salad and other ingredients Melissa needed.

"I think Jake would go crazy for help like this in the kitchen," Sunny stated as he stood in the small doorway. The kitchen was really tight, yet everyone worked together doing specific jobs. Even Tommy got plastic cups and plastic plates for the kids. Lea got the ceramic dishes for her, Melissa, him, and their aunt. Melissa smiled at his remark, and then a sad look covered her face.

He wished he knew what she was thinking.

* * * *

Melissa whipped up a delicious meal Sunny was certain that his brothers would love. He imagined her sharing recipes with Jake and maybe arguing over how to do it and whose way was better. He also imagined her displayed on their table again, but this time as dessert. He stuck around afterwards as she read the kids a story, got everyone washed up and ready for bed, then tended to her aunt.

He waited in the living room looking at family pictures, trying to get a hold on who Melissa really was.

* * * *

"He seems very nice for such a large man."

Melissa smiled at her aunt as she pulled down the covers on her aunt's bed.

"Not many men are as big as him or have such stunning eyes," she stated when Melissa didn't respond.

"He's just a friend." Melissa helped her aunt get into bed.

"I'm feeling stronger every day, Mel. Pretty soon you can go out on real dates instead of sneaking off."

Melissa swallowed hard. She hadn't snuck off. She had been taken into custody. It would have been worse if she had been caught stealing that money.

"I didn't sneak off. I was caught up at the job late and I was too tired to drive home. Celine's apartment is closer."

"You don't have to lie to me. I can see the pain in your eyes and the secrets you hold. Once the kids are in school tomorrow, we'll talk more about this and about Sunny."

"There's nothing to talk about. He's just a friend."

"I may have faced death in the eyes and be a considered a senior because I'm sixty-six years old, but I'm not blind. He cares for you, and you care for him."

"Goodnight," Melissa stated, trying to end the conversation.

"Goodnight, and be sure to give that handsome man a kiss goodnight from me, too."

Melissa giggled as she grabbed the pillow and blanket then headed out into the living room. She placed the pillow and blanket on the floor by the couch.

Sunny sat there smiling at her.

"What's the grin for?"

"My aunt wanted me to give you a goodnight kiss from her."

He smirked, then licked his lips.

"Come here," he whispered, and she went to him without hesitation.

He pulled her onto his lap and kissed her cheek. "That one is for Aunt Peggy."

Then he caressed her thighs and cupped her chin, tilting her head toward him.

"This one is all yours."

Before she could respond, Sunny kissed her. He squeezed her tighter as he explored her mouth with his tongue and cupped her breast. Immediately he sensed her arousal and knew he couldn't do anything about it.

Melissa pressed her hands against his chest, trying to end the kiss. When he released her lips, they were both breathless.

"You should go. I have to get the kids up for school tomorrow and I have a busy day with Celine."

"Then work tomorrow night?" he asked as he rose from the couch, still holding her in his arms.

She nodded her head.

"Please don't show up there, Sunny. I don't want any trouble. I need to make money. It's how I'm paying for everything."

He placed her on her feet and held her around her waist.

"No more stripping, right?" he asked and raised his eyebrows in warning.

She smirked. "No more stripping."

"Only for me and the guys, right?"

"Don't push your luck. Now get before the rest of the crew show up looking for you," she teased.

"They know I'm here. Wolves have great senses, baby." He kissed her then opened the door, saying goodnight one last time.

* * * *

Sunny exited the building, and the second he did, the wind blew, causing him to come to a halt. He sniffed the air and tried to act nonchalant. There was a wolf nearby. It was on the hunt or at least seemed like it was there waiting or hunting. He prepared for the attack as he approached his vehicle. He checked it over then contacted Logan.

Getting into the Jeep, he looked around the area.

"What do you think I should do?"

"Do you think this has something to do with our mate?" Logan asked.

"I'm not certain. My wolf is not happy about leaving Mel at all, never mind now that there's some stray wolf out there," Sunny responded.

"Frankie is on his way. Park the car a few blocks away and backtrack on foot to see who it is. Maybe you or Frankie will recognize him."

"Sounds like a plan," Sunny responded as he drove the Jeep down the road, making sure that no one followed him.

* * * *

"She's back home, sir. Arrived a couple of hours ago," Chu told Bret over the phone.

"Why didn't Felix grab her?" Bret asked, sounding irritated.

"She wasn't alone."

"Who was she with?"

"Sunny Valdamar."

"What?"

"It appears he stayed for the evening. Just left now alone."

"Shit. Do you think she's seeing him?"

"I smelt Valdamar on her in the club on Friday night, so if not Sunny, then with one of the others."

"Or all of them," Bret responded, sounding disgusted.

"What would you like me to have Felix do?"

"Get him out of there. It appears we have bigger problems. I'll handle Melissa tomorrow night. I need to figure out what angle she's working. I'm not so sure she's as innocent as she pretends. Or perhaps she's being pushed to be an informant. I wouldn't put it past the Valdamar or the rest of those pigs. Get Felix out of there pronto. If he smelled Valdamar and was that close, then Valdamar smelled him."

Chu hung up and immediately contacted Felix.

* * * *

"What do you think?" Sunny asked Frankie as he caught up with him behind the apartment complex."

"I think you scared the fucker off," Frankie replied.

"Good. Because my wolf is very uneasy about not being close to Melissa."

"So are the rest of ours as well. So what did you find out about her? You met the family? The kids?" Frankie asked, and Sunny explained about the small apartment, the two bedrooms and how Melissa sleeps on the couch. He told him about the pictures and the neighbor who Melissa had helped. He also talked about Brandon, Tommy, and Lea.

"The kids were that much fun, huh?" Frankie asked, sounding unsure.

"They were great. Very respectful and courteous. They helped with everything. Melissa's done a great job with them, I could tell."

"How was the food?" Frankie asked, and Sunny laughed.

"Jake has some serious competition."

"No shit?"

"No shit," Sunny replied as they laughed.

"Well, it looks like it's all clear."

"Then let's head home. Logan wants a rundown of my meeting the family and what I found out," Sunny stated. Then they headed back to his Jeep.

Chapter 13

"So what's the plan for tonight?" Chu asked Bret as Bret poured himself a snifter of brandy.

He turned toward Chu and smiled.

"Nothing."

Chu raised his eyebrows in response.

"I got a call from an inside guy about thirty minutes ago. He said Mel was asked to be an informant." He took a sip from his glass and smirked.

"What? Who the hell asked Mel to do that, fucking cops?"

Bret nodded.

"Son of a bitch. What did Mel say?"

"She downright refused."

"Smart woman. It would have been an instant death sentence."

"She knows that, Chu, but she also knows not to cross me. I can use this information on her. I can get her to cooperate with my demands."

"What about the Valdamar? They seem to like her a lot, and there are five of them."

"Fuck the Valdamar. I'll make her believe that they're the bad guys. I'll keep her away from them without physically having to do it. She won't know who to turn to. Especially if she thinks her kids and aunt are in danger."

Chu rubbed his chin.

"It could work. She knows you're of the wolf. She has to know that the Valdamar are. We could put a little scare into her, just to seal the deal."

"What are you thinking?"

"I've got some ideas. Give me some time to set it up. I'll let you know first and get your approval before I do anything."

"Sounds interesting, Chu. It's good to have a wolf of your resources on my side."

Chu chuckled.

"So we won't be headed to Charlie's tonight to visit?" Chu asked.

"No. We wait a few days and make our move."

* * * *

Melissa replied to the text messages from each of the guys. It had been one day and they acted as if it were a week. Releasing a sigh as she fixed her lip gloss in the bathroom at Charlie's, she admitted that she missed them, too. It was crazy to think how obsessed they each had become with one another. She longed to be held in their arms, kissed thoroughly by each of them, and of course made love to by them as well. But it wasn't love. She had to remind herself that it was lust, infatuation, and a good time for now. Eventually they would grow tired of her. They would find some other woman to shower with affection and send into a fantasy world that could never last forever.

She took a deep, unsteady breath and exited the bathroom.

Charlie was there waiting for her.

"You look beautiful, Melissa. Like a woman in love," he teased her. She lowered her eyes and shook her head. "No, not a woman in love."

"Well, they're your mates, and it's the same thing as when humans fall in love. It's just more intense for wolves."

She was shocked at his words. "Mates? What are you talking about? What do you mean?"

Charlie looked like he lost all the coloring on his face.

"Ah...I take it they didn't explain how it works."

"Uh, no, not if you're talking about anything having to do with wolf culture. They haven't explained anything."

"Well, maybe it's best if you ask them. I just assumed since you were with them that you were beginning the mating process."

"Oh crap, Charlie. I have no idea what the hell you are talking about." She moved closer and whispered despite the fact that no one was even in the club yet except for Spike and the workers who were in the other part of the club.

"Do you mean the sex?"

Charlie placed his hands in his pockets and seemed to blush.

"Ah, listen, honey, I think it's best if you talk to the guys. The only information I know is from my cousin. She is mated to two wolves, and there was this whole mating process. They united and once he and his brother bit her during sex, their bond was formed."

Melissa placed her hand over her shoulder where the bite marks were. Not all the brothers had bitten her yet.

"Did they bite you Mel?"

"Not all of them."

"Well, you're not truly bonded until they all mark you their mate. It's for security, protection, and a symbol of their love and commitment to you."

She thought about that a moment and remembered something the guys said.

"They mentioned a mating musk. What's that?"

"My cousin said it's what told her she belonged to her two men. She couldn't go long periods of time without them by her side. At least until the mating process was complete. When wolves mate, they mate for life."

"For life?" She panicked. What about the kids, her aunt, her life?

Suddenly she felt her blood boiling.

"They had no right to begin this," she stated as she began to pace the hallway. "I can't believe this is happening. I won't let this happen."

"You don't have much of a choice, Mel." He laughed.

"I do, too. I have a choice. I have a say in this. My whole life will change."

Charlie took her hand and smiled at her.

"Your life has already changed, Mel. You are glowing and in love. So stop fighting it and enjoy it."

In love? What the heck was he talking about?

"I'm not in love."

"Listen, I think you should talk this over with your men. They can better explain this than I can. Now let's get ready for a busy night. I have a new girl starting since you won't be dancing anymore."

"Says who?" she asked.

"You did, and I've been thoroughly warned by an entire SWAT team as well."

"Great. And so the controlling begins," Melissa stated as she sighed in anger.

* * * *

Melissa worked the bar and ignored every text she received until about midnight. Glancing down at her phone as she finished serving a group of businessmen martinis, she saw that it was Vince. For some strange reason, she had a soft spot for Vince. He just seemed so sincere and up front. He didn't hide things, and maybe that's why she was hurt that they hadn't explained the whole mating thing before they just did it.

Mel, call me please. I know something is wrong. I can feel it. Call or text me now. Vince

Great, now he could sense her emotions from afar. Could he sense her anger, too?

She pulled her cell phone off her hip and stared at the people around the bar and in the club. It just wasn't the same anymore. She was beginning to feel lost, and it was all because of the men.

She took a moment to text him.

I'm mad at you. I'm mad at your brothers, too. You should have explained and asked me first. Maybe I don't want to be mated.

As she pressed "send," her heart ached. If she were at all honest with herself, she would realize that she wanted to be with them. She was falling in love with them.

Instead of a text, her phone rang. It was Vince.

"Tara, can you cover for me for a few minutes?" Melissa asked.

"Sure, honey. I hope that call puts a smile back on your face."

Melissa forced a small smile then answered the phone as she walked to the end of the bar and to a small doorway.

"Hello."

"Who told you?" Vince demanded to know.

"Does it matter? The point is that you didn't. Neither did your brothers."

"We're sorry you're upset, but things got out of control quickly. We didn't know if you were involved with the case against Bret. We also felt compelled to have you. It's new for all of us as well."

"To have me, huh? That sounds romantic," she stated sarcastically.

"If you want romantic, we can do romantic. Wolves are sexual creatures. We like to make love to our women thoroughly and waste no time with the other stuff. Are you really that angry with us that you avoided our texts?"

"Yes. I'm hurt, that's all."

"Well, that's not acceptable. We would never hurt you. What time are you finishing up?"

"I don't know. It's kind of a slow tonight."

"Can you meet us at our place?"

She thought about it a minute. Aunt Peggy had Alice next door to help if she needed it. That woman was practically over at the apartment for coffee every morning anyway.

"Okay. I suppose I can, but I want to talk."

She heard the muffled cries and wise-guy comments of the others in the background.

"Call me or text me when you're leaving there."

"Okay."

Melissa hung up the phone, and for some reason, she felt a little better. If she were honest with herself, she would admit that she was excited about seeing her men again.

* * * *

She returned back to the bar to find a new guy waiting to be served.

Tara came up to Melissa and whispered to her, "He was asking for you. Wanted to wait for you to serve him. I think he's a cop."

She swallowed hard then slowly walked toward the tall blond-haired guy. He was big and quite attractive.

"Melissa?"

"And you are?"

"I'm Special Investigator Declan. I was just by your apartment a couple of hours ago. I met your family. Very nice kids."

"What is this all about, detective?" she asked, moving closer to the bar.

He leaned closer, and it seemed like he sniffed her. Great, was he a wolf too? Suddenly there seemed to be a lot of wolves around her.

He was hesitant as he spoke.

"I'm with the DEA. During an investigation into a recent drug operation bust, a large amount of money was stolen. We've tracked down some of the bills. However, it seems that some have wound up in an account with your name. Any ideas how that money got there?"

Oh shit!

"Um, I have no idea. I mean, I pretty much work here all the time. Different people come in and leave tips."

He looked her body over and hesitated as if contemplating his next comment.

"You've got a hot body. But thirty grand worth of dough in one night, I'm not buying."

"I don't know what you're inferring, Investigator Declan, but I don't know anything about any drug raid. But as far as the money, I just deposit any cash I get here into that account."

He looked her over again and sniffed the air. He smirked.

"Normally, I would believe a story such as yours. However, after further investigation by my team, it appears your friend Celine Lewis had a large sum of money in her account. Which came directly from your account, by the way."

"I've been saving my money for years. What's your point?"

He leaned forward so only she could hear.

"My point is that you've come into a lot of money in a short period of time. I'm not certain how exactly yet, but I do know stripping and bartending doesn't bring in that kind of cash in less than two weeks. There are numerous drug dealers that hang around this club. Perhaps they've offered you financial freedom so you can take care of your dead sister's kids and dying aunt. I'm not sure. What I do know is that these individuals are going down. The illegal drugs, the transporting and distributing of drugs, will come to an end. Are you going to be part of the problem or part of the solution?"

She stared at him, uncertain if his statement was a direct threat or if he was fishing for clues. She covered her tracks, and despite the marked bills, how the hell would he know that unless he illegally went to the bank and investigated? He was taking a chance on a hunch, nothing more.

She leaned back closer to him and smiled.

"This is all very interesting on hearsay. However, in order to prove that any individual has deposited money that is marked, that person would have to be present at the time of that deposit. If by chance they weren't, and they were guessing, then that person would have to get a warrant to look at the registers at that particular bank and verify a timetable, a location, and a precise register and teller that received those marked bills.

"Are you standing here telling me that you have done all of the above and have proven that I, amongst the thousands of people who use Wells Fargo bank on Main Street and Fifth Avenue, am the one person who deposited that marked money? Because there are very wealthy people who deposit money there in larger sums than thirty thousand. Plus, I only had about twenty thousand dollars that I moved from one account to another. That twenty thousand dollars was in singles, fives, and change. Hence, tips from the bar and tips from stripping every now and then. You'd be surprised what people tip a good stripper. So please don't waste my time on a cop hunch and think that I'm stupid."

He stared at her, and a small grin touched his face.

"I'm giving you a warning, miss. This is an ongoing investigation, and in the end you'll want to be on the good side, not the bad."

He winked at her then got up and left.

* * * *

Logan was sitting in the kitchen with his brothers waiting for Melissa to call when his phone rang. It wasn't her.

He took the call then left the room.

"What is a Declan calling him for? Is Task Force three part of this investigation now, too?" Frankie asked.

"It's a pretty big case, and they are a lead pack in the drug task force. Any recon would be done by them initially," Sunny suggested

"Oh yeah, I forgot about all that shit. Surveillance, special operations, they're a young bunch of wolves in those three teams," Vince acknowledged.

"Son of a bitch! You're not going to believe this," Logan yelled as he came storming back into the kitchen.

"What's wrong?" Jake asked.

"Melissa. She lied to us," Logan stated then began to explain about the money and Declan's investigation.

"So you think she stole the money from Bret, that's why she was at the warehouse the other night?" Jake asked.

"It looks like that's the case."

"Holy crap how the hell did she pull that off?" Frankie asked.

"She's in serious trouble here," Logan stated.

"What actual proof do they have?" Jake wanted to know.

Logan told them about the conversation between Melissa and Declan.

"She's quick on her toes, and more than likely she was right. He can't prove anything. The problem is that they're looking into her friends and the family. Declan scented wolf on the kids just like you did, Sunny," Logan added.

"Melissa probably doesn't know they have wolf blood. What did you find out about her brother-in-law Mike?" Vince asked.

"Nothing yet. Once Vince got the text from Melissa, then the call, I've been waiting for her to get here just like the rest of you," Sunny replied.

"Well, start looking into that. It could be of importance at a later date," Logan added.

"You mean to seal the deal with our mate?" Vince asked.

"Unless she winds up in prison," Frankie responded sarcastically.

They were all quiet for a moment as they pondered over that statement.

"Declan was giving us the heads-up. He could have pushed further. You all know he can be persuasive," Logan added.

"Were his brothers with him?" Vince asked.

Logan shook his head.

"Thank the gods," Jake added.

"Something tells me that our little dancer can be quite resourceful. Let's see how she handles our own kind of interrogation," Sunny stated with a gleam in his eyes.

"Finally, you're thinking like me, Sunny," Frankie replied sarcastically.

"What are you talking about?" Sunny asked.

"I wanted to give her ass a nice spanking for doing that striptease she did Friday night, and another one for being a potential suspect. That would have made her talk," Frankie stated confidently.

"You're so full of shit. You were thinking the same thing as the rest of us since the moment that we realized our Mel was the same woman as the dancer on that stage. Fuck and mate, fuck and mate," Jake replied, and the rest of them agreed.

"Tonight is going to have to be handled a little differently. First we need to explain what being our mate means. Next we need to get her to tell us the truth about Saturday night. Then we can seal our bond," Vince added, and they all agreed.

* * * *

Chu closed up his cell phone and locked gazes with Bret.

"One of the Declan brothers paid Melissa a visit."

"What? Why would he do that?"

"He questioned her about money in her account. Now Jamie is there. Melissa is getting ready to leave for the night."

Bret thought about the information.

"Is she working tomorrow?"

Chu nodded.

"Don't do anything tonight. I want you to find out why Declan is snooping around. I want to know what connections Melissa has to this.

"Do you think she was the one that stole the money from Lester?"

Bret's eyes began to glow then a smile formed on his lips.

"She knows the run. I never would have suspected her. She is definitely more resourceful than I'd give her credit for. She'll pay for that if it turns out she in fact did the hit. Right now find out everything you can. Also see if you can find out why Jamie is sniffing around."

"Yes, sir," Chu stated then walked out of the office.

* * * *

Melissa was leaving when Jamie met her by the exit.

"Hey, you done for the night?"

"Oh, hi, Jamie. Yeah, all finished."

"I was going to buy you a drink."

"No, thank you. I have plans."

"With the Valdamar brothers?" he asked.

She was taken aback by his question.

"I really need to get going," she replied and stepped through the doorway. She walked to her car, and that's when Jamie grabbed her hand. She felt him squeeze it tight then pin her against the car.

"I was talking to you, Mel. You don't walk away from me while I'm talking to you."

Melissa was shocked. She wondered what had come over Jamie to make him grab her like this. He was angry, and she had never seen him this way before.

"Let go of me, Jamie."

He pressed his body against hers, placing his hand on her hip bone.

He stared into her eyes then reached up to caress her cheek.

"You look so much like Sarah. You share the same eyes, the same sensual lips." He inched closer, and she couldn't help but fear his next move. He spoke about her sister as if he knew her intimately.

"How could you remember that? She's been dead for two years."

He caressed her cheek and pressed his thumb against her lips, making them part. She didn't want to move. In fear she licked her lips and accidentally hit his thumb.

"You don't belong with men like the Valdamars. Just like Sarah didn't belong with Mike."

"What are you saying? You were their friend. You were real close to Mike."

"I was close to Mike so I could be close to Sarah. She was too good for his kind. But she wouldn't leave him for me. She was scared of her own husband. She was afraid he would hurt her or maul her when he lost control of his body."

Was he saying that Mike was a wolf?

"What are you saying?"

He squeezed her face and made her look into his eyes.

"You don't belong with them, just like you don't belong to Bret."

His hold remained firm, and she couldn't get away from him. She attempted to turn her face, but his fingers dug into her cheek and chin. They would surely leave a mark. She needed to calm him down.

"Why did you come to see me tonight? I told you that I won't be a snitch. I have the kids to worry about, Jamie. You know I wouldn't take the chance."

He lightened his grip on her chin, but he pressed his groin harder against her belly. She felt his cock through his pants. This wasn't good.

Jamie caressed her lower lip then looked down at her cleavage.

"You're so sexy, Mel. You're all woman, and you shouldn't be working in a place like this. I can take care of you. I can take care of the kids."

"That's really kind of you, Jamie, but I couldn't let you do that. I couldn't lead you to believe that there's anything more than just friendship between us."

"No. Don't say that when you haven't even given me a chance. I won't go through this a second time. You don't belong to the Valdamar brothers. You belong to me, a human male. Don't make the same mistake Sarah did."

"What mistake would that be?"

"Choosing a freak like Mike over a real man like me."

Her heart pounded in her chest. Jamie was talking crazy. He made it sound like he was in love with Sarah, that they shared some sort of romance behind Mike's back, and that she chose Mike over him.

"I can't be responsible for decisions my sister made, Jamie. I really don't understand any of this. The truth of the matter is that I'm not seeing the Valdamar brothers. I just met them a few nights ago."

He squinted his eyes and pressed his body firmer against the car. She felt trapped and unable to move as he locked gazes with her.

His fingers caressed her neck and chin.

"But you're fucking them, aren't you? Just like Sarah was fucking Mike in between sleeping with me." He practically growled his last words he was so angry.

She wasn't certain which part of his statement she should challenge. Bringing the attention away from her would probably be best since no one was coming out of the building to interrupt this crazy situation. She was shocked at his statement.

"You had an affair with Sarah while she was with Mike?"

He was silent as he continued to caress her skin.

"The biggest mistake she made was choosing him over me. Look what it cost her. Both their lives."

Before she could respond or gasp in shock at his insinuation, he covered her mouth and kissed her. She tried to free her lips and pressed her hands against his chest, but he was on a mission to get his fill. His hands groped her body. He grabbed her breast and squeezed it rather hard until finally she was able to move her knee and lift it hard and fast enough to his groin. Jamie immediately pulled from her mouth, and she kicked him again then smacked his face.

"How dare you touch me? How dare you try to manhandle me? Get the hell out of here, or I swear I'll press charges."

"You can't do shit. You're the one who's going to jail, unless you end up having an accident just like Mike and Sarah."

He grabbed her neck and shoulder, pulling her toward him as he squeezed really hard. Melissa gasped and had to bend her body from the pain.

"This isn't over. We're going to be together, or I'll kill you and the Valdamars just like I killed Mike and Sarah." He shoved her as he released her neck, and she fell to the ground by her car. She scraped her knee and felt the pain in her shoulder and neck as she cried.

"This is my last warning, Mel. Stop seeing them and come to your senses or else. They're no good for you. They'll lie to you, use your body the way they want, and then they'll kick you to the curb. I won't take you back then. It's now or never."

Jamie walked away, leaving her there to think about what he just admitted to and what he wanted from her.

He killed them? *Oh my God, what do I do?*

She hurried to her feet, got into the car, and locked the doors. The tears rolled down her cheeks as she thought about everything Jamie had said. The affair, the fact that Mike was a wolf, and that Sarah had slept with Jamie. Was this some kind of sick joke? A few days ago she had no idea that were wolves truly existed, and now she was caught in the middle of some insane werewolf love triangle. The son of a bitch admitted to killing her sister and Mike. How could she prove this? Who could she talk to and trust with this? Her body shook, and she felt the stinging in her elbow.

Immediately she thought of the brothers. She had texted them as soon as she was ready to leave the club. That was a while ago. They were probably worried. She couldn't tell them about Jamie, or they would be angry and go after him. She didn't want that on her conscience. She would find a way to get him back. She had to. Her hands were shaking as she tried to place the key into the ignition. After a few attempts, she was successful in starting the car.

Then she thought about the brothers. What if Jamie was right? What if they only wanted to use her then toss her away? She felt her heart ache, and she began to cry. What should she do? Feeling conflicted and still shocked at Jamie's confession, Melissa felt helpless. She wanted to vomit. Yet something was pushing her to be with the brothers. Was it the mating bond that she and Charlie had spoken about? Was it too late to turn back? Did they already have a hold of her? She swallowed the lump of emotions in her throat. She thought about Jamie. He would hurt her family. How could she protect them from him? The kids? He said that Mike was a wolf. Did that mean the kids had wolf blood in them? She knew nothing of their culture. She hadn't noticed any signs of them being different. She didn't know what to do. This was all over the top for her.

She sat there letting the tears fall as she debated about where to go. Her cell phone rang making her jump. She was a nervous wreck. Jamie could have forced himself on her or worse.

"Hello."

"Is everything all right? We're worried," Sunny stated through the phone.

His strong voice penetrated her heart, and although he was angry, it made her feel safe. She couldn't believe it as the tears rolled down her cheeks, and her throat felt as if it clogged up.

"Mel? Mel, answer me." His voice got louder, but she began to cry as the words tumbled from her mouth.

"I can't."

"Are you okay? Where are you?"

She cried as the tears flowed and an overwhelming need for her men replaced the fear.

"I'm on my way," she stated in a shaky voice then disconnected the call.

She tossed her phone into her open purse and prayed she hadn't made the wrong decision. Her family's lives depended on it.

* * * *

When she made it down their private road with no cars following her and to the bend before their long driveway, she could see their houses in the distance and all five men waiting for her by the front walkway.

She parked the car as Sunny got to her first.

She practically jumped into his arms. He squeezed her to him, and she closed her eyes and relished the safety of his arms.

Chapter 14

Sunny and his brothers sensed Melissa's fear, but Sunny also smelled men's cologne and another man's saliva on her neck. He walked her inside with his brothers, and they entered the living room.

They all took in the sight of her, but Sunny's eyes remained on her neck and the red marks.

It was Frankie who touched his fingers to her skin.

"Who did this to you?' They watched as tears rolled down her cheeks.

* * * *

Logan didn't know what happened, but whatever it was, it put a fear in Melissa. He could hear her heart racing, and her body was tense.

"Enough! Tell us what happened now!" Logan yelled, and his brothers looked at him then back at Melissa. She stood in front of the couch with her hands clasped in front of her. Her shoulders sagged, the tears ran down her cheeks, and finally her legs gave out as she fell to the couch into a sitting position. Melissa covered her face with her hands.

"I don't know where to start. I don't know if this is right."

Immediately Vince was kneeling in front of her caressing her thighs.

"Calm down and take nice steady breaths," he whispered, and she looked up at him. She stared at him in a way that showed conflict and desire. They could all see it.

Vince cupped her cheek where the red marks stood out, and she leaned into his hand.

"I can't stop shaking."

Vince pulled her to him, pressing his thighs between her legs, causing her to straddle his waist as he embraced her. He caressed her back, and she seemed to calm down a bit.

"Who scared you?" Sunny demanded to know.

"What will you do if I tell you?"

"Rip the fucker's throat out," Frankie replied then smirked at Melissa. He, too, was trying to calm her down.

She chuckled between a snort, then pulled a little away from Vince.

Vince continued to caress her thighs as she looked at each of them.

* * * *

"First of all, trust doesn't come easy for me. I've been on my own for a while, and leaning on others hasn't been an option. But I'm following my gut here. I want to trust you despite the fact that none of you were upfront about the whole wolf mating thing."

"Sometimes the wolf's needs overpower the man's control," Jake offered with a smile, letting his eyes roam over her body. Instantly her nipples hardened and her pussy leaked. The men inhaled.

"Keep that up and talking will be over for a while," Frankie stated. He was such a tease. Their bold brown eyes held her gaze, and she knew in her heart that they would never hurt her.

Taking a deep breath, she began to explain what happened this evening and what Jamie had revealed to her.

They did not interrupt her, but their eyes changed color, and their demeanor changed. They were angry that Jamie had hurt her and had threatened her.

Vince took a seat on the couch and pulled her into his arms. She straddled his hips and cried as she revealed her fears to them.

"He told me that you would use me then get rid of me when you were done having your way."

"That fucking piece of shit. I'll rip out his jugular the second I get the chance," Sunny stated.

"He lied to you, Melissa. He wants you to fear him. They're all lies. We'll protect you and your family."

Melissa felt Vince's hands caress her lower back, then her thighs. She loved the feel of his hands on her. She wanted all of them, but she was skeptical.

"He killed my sister and her husband. I'm afraid. I'm scared that he will hurt the kids."

Logan moved behind her. She felt his hands on her shoulders as he massaged her tense muscles. She looked up at him.

"The kids are of the wolf. They will be protected by wolves from here on out, and we will get to the bottom of this."

"They don't show signs of being of the wolf, as you say. How can we be sure?" she asked them.

Jake now stood behind the couch and Vince's head as he spoke to her.

"Sunny met them at your apartment. Their scent indicated that they were of the wolf. Your brother-in-law was a member of the Paruva pack. They're related to Declan," he stated, and she felt her insides coil up tight, and her body stiffened at the name.

The investigator who came to the bar tonight was a wolf, and his last name was Declan.

Logan squeezed her shoulders, and she swallowed hard.

"We're ready to protect you and help you, Melissa, but you have to be honest with us. Were you involved with the drug deal near the warehouse we busted the other night?"

She felt sick to her stomach and guilty for her actions but not regretful.

"I wasn't involved with the drug deal or the warehouse. I was responsible however for stealing the money that was going to be used to buy the drugs."

She kept her head down until Vince placed his fingers under her chin and made her look at him.

"Why did you do it?"

She took a deep, unsteady breath as a tear fell from her eye. Then she stared at Vince, then Jake and Frankie who stood behind him. Sunny and Logan remained behind her.

This was the hardest thing she ever had to do and admit to. They could take her to jail. They could make her return the money or worse. They could hate her.

"I needed the money, and so did some friends."

"What do you mean you needed the money? There was more than a hundred thousand dollars in that bag," Sunny stated from the side of her.

"One hundred and fifty thousand to be precise," she replied, and Frankie whistled.

"What did you do with the money?"

She began to explain about Celine's situation and the banker. She went on about the food shelter and then the families in her building. She talked about Alice losing two children to foster care and how Melissa worked the system to get them back.

"This wasn't the only hit you did, was it, Mel?" Jake asked her, and she shook her head. Then she began to tell them about the money she stole to give back to the hospital's fundraiser and her aunt's surgery. She explained about the clinic and how her aunt almost died then about giving up her last bit of money she had saved for college so she could legally adopt the children and afford the apartment. She found herself explaining about taking the job with Bret and getting the job at Charlie's.

"Everything you've done and sacrificed has been for the sake of everyone else but you, Melissa. What did *you* get out of all this?" Frankie asked.

"It wasn't about me. It was about them. All of them. I can't fail those kids or my aunt. I can't sit back and let my friend, my neighbors suffer and do nothing. Bret is a slimeball, and sure, I made a mistake getting involved with him, but it gave me the insight I needed to pull everything off. I don't regret any of it. I took from a group of worthless, heartless drug dealers that destroy and kill children, adults, and families with their poison. Bret has more money than you can imagine. He didn't have a clue I was responsible."

"You could have been killed, then what?" Vince replied to her statement, his anger apparent by his glowing eyes and the forceful way he clutched her hand.

"It was a chance I was willing to take. Have you ever been so hungry or so scared that you were desperate for anything, even the smallest crumb or the tiniest bit of warmth? Probably not, because you're wolves. I was desperate, and I was all alone. I had no choice, and I would do it again in a heartbeat."

"What you did was illegal, and there are consequences for that," Logan stated as he caressed her hair. She felt the tiny pricks of fear and arousal travel down her spine and straight to her cunt. The man was a lethal force.

She tilted her head up so she could look him in the eye.

"Prove it."

His eyes glowed, and he looked menacing in his position.

"Declan has proof that can put you away for life," Sunny replied.

"Declan doesn't have shit. I wasn't born yesterday, you know. I've covered my tracks well, and nothing he could get would stand up in a court of law," she replied confidently.

"In a human court of law, no, but as wolves and as your mates, there must be a punishment for these crimes," Logan told her, tugging her hair a bit harder.

Her head tilted back, and she nearly lost her balance, but his thighs held her back in place as Vince caressed her inner thighs and under her skirt.

Her chest rose and fell. She knew he had a perfect view of her breasts and cleavage. Her nipples hardened and pressed against the fabric of her lace bra.

"What kind of punishment?" she asked in a husky voice that came out way sexier than she intended.

"You'll see," Logan whispered then leaned down and covered her mouth with his own. His tongue dueled with hers for a moment, and her body swayed as Vince lifted her and began removing her skirt. The sound of her panties ripping, then the cool air caressing her pussy sent her body up in flames.

* * * *

Logan had a multitude of emotions. He was angry that his mate was a criminal. He was proud at her ability to evade capture and to help the needy like she had done. He was impressed with her selflessness, and he feared for her life. As her mates, he and his brothers were now responsible for her. The criminal activities had come to an end now, and he hoped that they could get her out of the trouble she was currently in. But at this moment, the scent of her arousal, the taste of her mouth and her skin, as well as the feel of her curves was calling his and his brothers' wolves.

Logan lifted Melissa from around the waist and raised her enough for Vince to pull down his pants and remove them.

He squeezed her breasts, making sure to fondle each mound then tweak the hardened nubs.

He felt his wolf burn with need to fuck its mate. It was angry at her indiscretions, and out of all the information Melissa had shared, his wolf was pissed that she had fucked Bret.

He released her lips and held her gaze as she straddled Vince but remained on her knees above Vince's cock.

His brother Vince continued to cup Melissa's breasts then lick her nipples, first one then the other.

He spoke to his brothers through their link, and Vince lifted Melissa, positioning her to his liking. Vince laid on the couch with his legs over the low arm rest. He lifted Melissa then lowered her onto his cock.

Logan held a fistful of her hair in his hand and tugged. "Fuck your mate and bond with him fully. It's going to be a long, hard night for our little criminal." He tugged, and Melissa moaned as she caressed Vince's chest then thrust her hips back and forth then up and down over his cock.

* * * *

Melissa felt her cream drip from her pussy, all from Logan's commanding words. She didn't think she would be turned on by aggression, but right now she wanted them to punish her every which way they could and to take away her fear. She had been lost on her way here. She was unsure whether coming to the brothers' was the right thing to do or an even bigger mistake. But feeling Vince's thick cock move back and forth against her vaginal muscles, she felt safe, and she felt alive.

Logan pressed his large hand against her spine, trailing a finger up and down each bump as Vince pulled her nipples. Logan pressed her lower, giving Vince the opportunity to lick and suck on her sensitive breast.

Her body orgasmed as tiny vibrations rocked her insides. She thrust her hips up and down faster, her pussy clenching Vince's cock and taking him deep. She was caught up in the need for him, for cock, and for the connection she felt. When Logan pressed a finger to her anus she screamed another release.

Melissa was on fire. Now she felt a strong pull to have all her men. She looked up and saw Sunny, Frankie, and Jake standing around the couch watching her.

She held each of their gazes.

"You belong to us, Mel. Feel the connection, and feel our desire for you," Jake spoke as he approached the couch. He caressed her cheek, and her eyes zeroed in on his very large, long cock. He held it in his fist and touched it to her lips. She saw the pre-cum on the mushroom tip, and when she went to lick it off, she received a hard slap to her ass.

She screamed softly at the unexpected blow.

Simultaneously, Vince pinched and pulled her nipples as Logan pressed a finger to her anus, pushing right through the tight ring of muscles. Melissa panted for air, trying to catch her breath at the onslaught of sensations rocking her body. She pushed her ass back against Logan's finger, causing her to receive another smack to her ass.

"We're running the show, sweetheart. Your punishment begins now." Logan growled then smacked her ass again just as Jake gently grabbed a fistful of her hair and stared at her.

"Open those sexy, wet lips of yours, baby, so I can cleanse that mouth," Jake stated as Logan pulled his finger from her anus. She moaned and opened her mouth. Jake pressed his hard, thick cock between her parted lips, and she sucked as much of him inside as she could. He rocked his hips back and forth, causing his cock to slide in and out of her mouth. Vince thrust his hips up and down, and she could feel his cock growing harder and longer as he fucked her pussy. Another slap to her ass and she screamed a release, causing a gush of fluid to leak from her cunt. Vince slid in and out of so fast, that she held on to his shoulders, gripping them tight. It was difficult to keep her mouth around Jake's cock, sucking him with all she had while they infiltrated her body She never expected the next move by Logan. As soon as she felt the tip of his cock at her back entrance, she sucked

Jake harder, causing him to yank at her hair and caress her cheek. Vince slowed his pace, and Logan pushed forward, his cock feeling enormous as he pushed through the tight rings of her back hole and caused her to fall against Vince's chest. Strong arms and hands wrapped around her. Fingers pulled, pinched, and caressed every inch of her body as three of her wolves made love to her. She felt dizzy with desire and as if she were in some sort of fantasy dream at all the sensations.

She wanted to touch Jake and feel the muscles of his chest beneath her fingertips, but if she released her hold on Vince, she would fall.

Jake moaned as he closed his eyes then held her head in place as he pumped his seed down her throat and filled her with his essence. She swallowed as quickly as she could. The warm liquid flowed down her throat while Vince shoved his cock up into her pussy. Up and down, he gripped her hip bones, making her stay stationary. Over and over he pumped into her. She was lost in the feel of his balls against the crevice of her ass where Logan's cock remained deep within her. The double friction caused another onslaught of spasms to explode inside of her. Vince shoved up one more time then pulled her toward him, covering her mouth with his own as he exploded inside of her.

Logan began to pump and thrust into her ass as he grabbed her hips and lifted her rear. Her breasts were pressed against Vince's chest as she gasped for air while Logan fucked her ass from behind. Over and over again he pressed his hips, causing deeper penetration until suddenly, the smack to her rear came out of nowhere. She screamed her release as Logan pumped and pumped and pumped against her, shoving her breasts against Vince's chest. Vince held her hair and widened his legs, causing Logan to go even deeper until finally he growled his released and pumped his seed inside her. Logan lifted her from Vince, wrapped his arms around her waist as he cupped her breast, and gave a few more strokes. They panted for air.

Logan slowly pulled from her body, kissing her neck, her shoulder, and then her back before she felt the next set of hands on her.

* * * *

Frankie turned Melissa toward him and kissed her wildly. It had been torture to watch his brothers fuck their mate. He wanted his turn, and so did Sunny. The sound of Melissa's moans as Logan spanked her ass had nearly caused Frankie to come just from watching her.

Frankie lifted her in the air, and she straddled his hips. The feel of her plump breasts against his chest made him weak with desire. Her pussy felt moist and ready for his cock as the wetness hit his belly. He released her lips and kissed her neck, biting and nibbling until he found her breast. His hands lifted her higher as his fingers grazed her cunt.

"You're wet for me, baby. I can feel your moist pussy. You're perfect," he stated before pulling part of her breast into his mouth and sucking it hard.

He felt Melissa's hands running up and down his shoulders then over his neck and through his hair. He was on fire with need. He had to have her. His cock throbbed and banged up against her wet folds and back entrance.

Frantically he looked around the room and sought out the desk where some papers and the computer sat. With one arm, he shoved everything off the desk then planted her perfect ass on top of it. Fisting his cock in his hand, he stared at her a moment.

She was gorgeous. A small patch of red blush covered her chest between her cleavage. Her lips were parted, her cheeks were flushed, and her hair was wild from her sexual tussle with Logan, Jake, and Vince.

There was just enough room for her to lie back as he lined his cock with her pussy and shoved forward. The sound of his Melissa moaning and the feel of her nails grabbing at his body sent him into frenzy. She belonged to them, and right now his wolf was set to fuck and claim her.

Pulling her legs by his side, he gradually increased his speed. His cock was so fucking hard, and her inner muscles clenched his cock and sent him to near ejaculation.

"Fuck, Mel, you feel so fucking good. You're so tight and hot inside. My cock can hardly move."

"It's fucking incredible, isn't it," Vince chimed in.

Melissa moaned and reached up to press her hands against his pectoral muscles. As she pinched the pink flesh, he lost control. He lifted her legs higher so he could penetrate her deeper, then began a series of deep, hard thrusts that rocked the desk top. Things started falling off the top piece behind Melissa's head and onto the floor behind the desk, but he didn't care. His wolf wanted more.

Over and over he thrust his cock, feeling her muscles hold him tighter, and he couldn't take anymore. One last thrust and he exploded inside of her, sending his seed deep within her and hopefully to her womb as he bit into her shoulder.

The thought scared the shit out of him. He was the one that didn't want any kids. He didn't want to settle down, and he wanted pussy for life with no commitments. That was until he met Melissa, his mate and hopefully the mother of his pups. He softly licked the wound and snuggled next to her.

Opening his eyes, he caught her stare, leaned down, and kissed her.

When he released her lips, the words shot from his tongue.

"I love you, mate. You're ours forever."

Her eyes widened, but then a tear fell from the corner of her eye. He lifted her from the desk top, hugged her close to his chest as he massaged her back.

* * * *

Melissa couldn't believe her ears, but she wanted to accept Frankie's words as the truth. She was in love with them as well. The realization hit her like a ton of bricks as she held on to Frankie.

Then she felt the large presence behind her and then lips to her neck.

"I need to love my woman, too," Sunny admitted then took her from Frankie's arms.

He cradled her in his arms as he carried her out of the room and upstairs to the bedroom.

* * * *

Sunny gently placed her on the bed then covered her body with his own. She returned his kisses. She loved the feel of his large, solid body on top of hers, encaging her in safety and love. She caressed his cheek as she looked into his dark brown eyes and saw his desire.

Running her fingers through his hair, she absorbed his beauty. He was built like some extra-large football player, but he was gentle as a lover should be. Her belly quivered from his stare and from his caress. She continued to explore his body, kissing his shoulder then pushing against him, indicating that she wanted him to roll to his back.

He allowed her to do as she wished with his body. Melissa absorbed his size and his muscles. He was intimidating-looking but also a beautiful sight. He appeared feast-like as he lay out before her. Nibbling her bottom lip she eyed him from firm lips to engorged cock. Although her pussy felt somewhat tender from her other lovers, she was interested in getting more.

"You gonna stare at me all night, or are you going to ride me, mate?" he asked, and her heart hammered inside of her chest. She kissed his lips then trailed more kisses along his chin, his neck, and to his chest. Every inch of him was manly and solid. Running her hands over the hard muscles, she pressed her breasts over his cock then straddled him better.

Sunny teased her.

"I love your tits, Mel. They're fucking perfect."

His face lit up, and she used that special look of Lilly's she used during dancing onstage to get the big tips. Sunny's brown eyes sparkled with specks of yellow. Sunny originally looked untamable to Melissa, but suddenly she felt like she had the ability to tame him.

She massaged her breasts and rocked her pussy against Sunny's hips. He grabbed a hold of her thighs and rubbed her skin back and forth, getting closer to her groin and pussy with each hand stroke.

She moaned then slid down his body, placing his cock between her cleavage and moving back and forth. Sunny moaned and spread his legs. His cock was so long and so thick that the mushroom top peeked out and she could lick it with her tongue.

"Oh, fuck!" Sunny moaned, trying to grab at her hair to gain some control. He slammed his fists down on the side of the bed as she continued to rub his cock back and forth between her breasts.

Suddenly she felt a slap to her ass, and she lifted up and turned behind her.

There was Jake with mischief in his eyes and sporting a thick, hard cock.

"Who's doing the punishing in here?" he teased as Sunny pulled Melissa up and shifted his body so that his legs lay over the side of the bed.

"Come here," Sunny told her as he cupped her breasts and gave them a tug. She leaned forward, catching his lips with her own and raising her ass in the air.

The second slap nearly did her in as she jolted forward against Sunny. He smirked as she felt the tip of his cock against her pussy. Her cream dripped from her cunt. It was a natural lubricant for Sunny's cock. Her body wanted him inside of her.

"Ride him," Jake demanded, and she lowered herself onto Sunny's shaft, taking him deep. He didn't have to tell her twice. Jake's stern tone totally turned her on.

She inhaled slowly, taking his steely, thick cock inside her inch by inch.

Her hips flexed and moved back and forth over Sunny, and she began a slow rhythm.

* * * *

Sunny was lost in ecstasy. He never experienced anything like this in his life, and he had a lot of lovers. He loved everything about Melissa. From her gorgeous looks to her perfect body all the way to her hot, wet cunt. Her vaginal walls gripped his cock and milked him. He could shoot his load right now, but he had to fight it. She was an exceptional lover, and he wondered how she learned the things she did. It made him angry, and he found himself asking something he never asked a woman before. Especially while his cock was deep in her pussy.

"Where did you learn how to be such a sensual lover?"

She slowed her rhythm above him, and he gave her hips a squeeze, silently indicating for her to continue.

"Are you asking me how many men I've had sex with?" she panted as she continued to thrust.

"I want to know."

"So do I," Jake said from behind her as he ran his hands over her back. Sunny knew his brother was going to fuck her ass. He told him through their link what he wanted to do to her. It added to Sunny's arousal.

"I've only had five lovers and one sexual fling."

His eyes widened at five until he realized what she had meant. Then he pulled her down and kissed her.

* * * *

Melissa nearly chuckled at teasing Sunny. She was shocked that he was asking her such a question in the middle of sex. For such macho Alpha males, it seemed she was gaining some power over them. Not that she would ever hurt them or use it against them, but it gave her confidence that this relationship might not be one-sided. That was one of her fears. Would the brothers want to control her every move and be their puppet? It wasn't worth the financial freedom or the security she had in their arms. She was too independent. But then she couldn't think a coherent thought as she felt Jake press his cock against her back entrance.

She felt him pull away then, and the disappointment made her exhale loudly. Sunny chuckled, but Jake rolled his tongue down her spine all the way to her crevice. He licked lower, catching the cream from her pussy and licking back over her back entrance. She moaned then thrust against Sunny's cock.

She inhaled then relaxed as he pushed his thick cock through the tight rings and into her body.

She was about to continue to ride Sunny when she felt Jake pull her arms up above her head and hold them there.

Her breasts pushed out in front of her where Sunny pulled and rubbed them thoroughly, and Jake thrust his cock in and out of her back entrance, making her pant for air.

She moaned at the sensations as her pussy wept with lust. She ground her pubic bone against Sunny's dick, taking him inside her while Jake fucked her from behind. Their rhythm increased until Sunny took over thrusting up into her in fast, hard upward thrusts. Jake pushed her down so she could be closer to Sunny.

Sunny covered her mouth and kissed her hard as he shoved his hips up and down.

She moaned, and her body tightened. Sunny thrust four more times then exploded inside of her, shooting his essence into her womb as he bit into her shoulder. Then she felt Jake grab her around the midsection, cover her breast with one hand, then pull her back against him. The move caused greater penetration as his hard cock thrust in and out of the tight rings until they both exploded together. Jake bit into her shoulder and pumped three more times until she felt herself falling toward Sunny.

Jake pulled from her body, and Sunny did the same then pulled her against his side.

Jake followed, climbing on the bed and taking position on her other side where he caressed her arm and shoulder.

"You're beautiful, Mel. That was amazing."

She was too tired to verbally respond and instead gave a content smile as she closed her eyes and fell asleep.

Chapter 15

Melissa got out of the shower and was grateful that the hot water eased her sore muscles. Her body had been overworked and parts that had never been used before now felt the repercussions. The thought of Logan and Jake slapping her ass caused an instant flow of wetness to her pussy. Her belly would tighten up, and shockingly, with just a little touch from one of her men, she would orgasm. This was exhilarating and frightening at the same time.

She dried her body off then wrapped the towel around her waist. Drying her hair, she thought about the kids and Aunt Peggy and decided to call them. She knew Alice was right across the hallway if they needed anything, but still she worried. Especially after what Jamie revealed last night.

Melissa used her cell phone as she leaned against the bathroom counter.

"Is everything okay?" she asked her aunt.

"Everything is fine. How are you?"

"I'm good. I should be home in a little while."

"There's no need to rush, Mel. Enjoy yourself. Celine is coming over for lunch, and Alice and I are making breakfast for the kids. They said to say hello to Sunny."

The tears stung Melissa's eyes. How the hell was she going to explain that she was in love with not one man but five men?

"Mel, are you okay?"

"Yes. I'll tell him, and I will see you later today. Thanks."

Melissa hung up the phone and looked at herself in the mirror.

Her cheeks were lightly pink, her complexion bright, and she looked happy. The men had completed her life, and yet here she was still feeling conflicted. How could she explain this to the kids and to her aunt?

"Mel, did you hear me?" The sound of Sunny's voice startled her. She clasped the towel around her body and stared up at him. Sunny looked sexy with his wet hair clinging to his shoulders and his sparkling brown eyes as he approached. His black shirt stretched across his muscles, making her heart hammer in her chest.

He placed his hands on her waist and stared down at her.

"Is everything okay? I thought I heard you talking on the phone."

She looked up and smiled.

"I called home. Everything is fine. The kids said hello."

He smiled at that, and her heart soared. Sunny was so nice to the kids that night he came over.

He placed his fingers under her chin and tilted it up toward him as he pressed her back against the counter.

"Then why the sad face?"

"Not sad, just confused."

"Talk to me and tell me what's going on."

She explained about the call and her feelings as well as what she would tell the kids.

"If they are of the wolf, like what we expect, considering that their father was wolf, then you'll have to explain things to them anyway. They'll need us to teach them about their heritage and their possible abilities."

"You mean they could shift one day like you?"

"It's quite possible. Lea is twelve, so she may be the first one. Brandon and Tommy have time."

She covered her face with her hands and exhaled.

"Hey, you're not alone in this. We're your mates, and this is for forever. But first there are some things you're going to have to help us with in order for us to keep you out of jail."

"What?" she asked, shocked.

"William Declan called and spoke with Logan a little while ago. He has enough proof to put you behind bars with the government's approval. He's willing to forget everything because of the reasons why you did it and because of your brother-in-law Mike. Logan negotiated for you, and because our packs are good friends with Declan's, we made a deal. It's all in good faith and trust between us weres. Declan knows that you're our mate and that we will do everything to protect you. He also knows what Jamie did to Mike, and he will be prosecuted. Let's get you dressed then come downstairs. Jake is preparing some breakfast in a little while, and the others are growing impatient to see you."

He leaned down and kissed her softly.

She was lost in the kiss as he pulled away, taking her towel with him.

"Sunny!" she exclaimed as she tried to cover her breasts with her arm and her pussy with her hand.

He gave her a stern look then eyed her from head to toe.

"Don't you hide from me, ever." He pulled her into his arms and kissed her some more then carried her out of the bathroom to the bedroom.

* * * *

Jake began cooking in the kitchen, making eggs and working side by side with Melissa. Every so often she would bump his hip and try to scoot him out of the way. They talked about some things she enjoyed cooking, recipes, and special traditions she tried to start with the kids.

"What did your sister and Mike teach them about their families?"

She looked down at the eggs cooking in the pan and prepared to add the fresh peppers, tomatoes, and cheese to the omelet.

"I asked them when they came to live with me, but they were still so fragile emotionally. The whole changing of schools, losing touch with their friends, and dealing with the loss of their parents was too much at once. As we came across holidays and special events, I just kind of started my own traditions with them."

Jake smiled as she shared her life with him. The more they spoke, the more he realized what a big heart she had.

"You did great with them, Mel. Any traditions you started and continue with them will one day be just as important to them and their families. I understand that it was difficult for you to take care of these kids at such a young age. You've accomplished so much, and you're only twenty-two."

She was silent a moment, and he wished that he knew what she was thinking. He wanted to protect her and give her the support she needed with her aunt and the kids. He and his brothers were already talking about redoing the other house on the property for her aunt to live in. They just didn't know how Melissa would react to it. There were a lot of adjustments to make and a lot to deal with the kids alone. Jake was confident it would work out. They gathered the food and set out the platters. Melissa was grabbing the orange juice out of the refrigerator when Logan, Sunny, and Frankie emerged.

"Let's eat then get this discussion going so we can make a plan," Logan stated as he pressed a hand to Melissa's then reached around her to take the orange juice container from her hands. He pulled out a chair. "Sit here," he told her, and she immediately did as he said and he smiled.

Jake took the seat next to her, and Frankie and Sunny sat across from her.

"Where's Vince?" she asked.

"He's on the phone confirming some information. He'll be here in a minute."

Jake wondered what was going on, and then Logan spoke to him through their link.

"Our mate was the one who miraculously saved the local food shelter when the food pantry was robbed last year. She's responsible for numerous anonymous donations made to shelters and children's foster care. She's been taking from the drug dealers and criminals for over a year and giving the money to the poor and the needy. Declan has interviewed a few of the neighbors. Some of them are were from Fidelis's pack who left their packs after being persecuted. We all know those stories from Lord Crespin and our cousins. Melissa had helped were-members without even knowing it."

"She's the one the news reporters have been talking about. Our mate is Robin Hood!" Frankie stated as he dropped his fork.

"That's Miss Robin Hood," Melissa responded, and everyone dropped their forks and stared at her.

Melissa continued to eat as if nothing had happened.

"Melissa!" Logan called to her, and she glanced up in shock at his tone. Slowly she put the fork down. Just then, Vince entered the room.

"What?"

"You just answered us in our minds. You heard our thoughts and responded," Logan exclaimed in shock.

"No, I didn't. I was just imagining what you were thinking and talking to myself in my head when—"

Melissa covered her mouth with her hand and gasped as she jumped up from the table.

Jake caught her around the waist before she took off.

"It's okay, Mel. This is normal, and it's a good thing," Vince added as he caressed her hair.

Melissa uncovered her mouth. "How can reading minds be normal? I didn't even know I was doing it. I don't understand this."

"Don't panic. Just sit down, and we'll explain it all," Logan attempted to calm her as Jake pulled her chair out and helped her to sit. Vince stood behind her massaging her shoulders as Logan explained the mating bond.

"So this is a good thing?" Melissa asked.

"It means that we're making progress and our bond is growing stronger. The more we make love to you and fill you with our seed and connect, the stronger our bond becomes," Logan explained then took a bite of a piece of bacon.

Melissa swallowed hard.

"How do I block it?" she asked, and Logan's eyes widened in shock. His brothers looked at her with just as much upset.

Then the little minx chuckled.

"For a bunch of big, intimidating men, you're so easy." Then she picked up her fork and began eating. Vince laughed out loud then made himself a plate and sat down beside Frankie.

They talked a little more about the mating bond and hearing one another's thoughts. Then they talked about the kids and their potential abilities. That's when Logan noticed that Melissa's eyes were tearing.

"Hey, what's wrong?" he asked then reached across her lap to take her hand into his own.

"We didn't use any protection. This is all so much to take in and I'm worried."

"Ah, baby, there's no need to worry about anything. You have five men who are your mates, your lovers and protectors," Logan offered in support.

"But I was hoping to finish my degree and take the bar exam. I wanted to become a lawyer. As soon as I saved enough money, I wanted to pursue that career. I need to save money for the kids for college, and working at the club is not going to be enough."

"And what makes you think that you can't?" Jake asked her, sounding insulted.

"I don't know. I thought maybe you guys expected me to stay at home. Maybe control my every move and be at your beck and call. You are Alphas right? Aren't I supposed to serve you?"

"Are you crazy? We don't want a puppet. We want a wife and a mate," Logan exclaimed.

"Yeah, and you'll have five men to help take care of the pups when they come along," Vince added.

"We'll work it all out, Mel. There's no need to worry anymore," Sunny firmly replied.

"You're not alone anymore, Mel. You've got us. I'm glad that you're talking in terms of staying and seeing this through. We're meant to be together," Jake stated.

Frankie stood up and walked around the table then caressed her hair as he looked into her eyes.

"We love you, Mel. It will all be fine, you'll see." He leaned down and kissed her lips softly then smiled.

"Okay. Now we have some business to discuss so we can keep our little Miss Robin Hood out of a jail cell," Logan commanded as he stood up from the table, taking his plate with him.

Chapter 16

Fifteen minutes later, William Declan and his four brothers showed up at the Valdamar brothers' home. Melissa was surrounded by monstrous yet drop-dead gorgeous men. The sight of them made her belly quiver and her eyes stick to absorbing every inch of their bodies. They knew it, too, as they stared right back at her as if she were their next meal.

Melissa was used to men looking her body over, but none besides the Valdamar brothers looked her over like these guys. She handled it well as she placed her hands on her hips and eyed them from boots to crew-cut heads.

One of the Declan chuckled. "You ready to back up that look there, dancer?" he asked, and she raised her eyebrows at him.

"You think you have what it takes, wolf?" she replied back, and the *oohs* and *ahhs* went through the room.

"Be careful, Mick, she's not easily intimidated," William Declan added as he took a seat on the couch and opened up a folder.

Melissa eyed the mouthy one, absorbing his blond hair and adorable dimples. He looked clean-cut yet mysterious. He shouldn't be underestimated either.

She felt a hand go around her waist then tap her hip bone.

"Take a seat next to Willy. He has some questions for you," Frankie told her, and she stared at Willy and his firm expression. That man was all business. As she walked toward the couch, Mick leaped over it and took a seat on the other side so she would be forced to sit between him and his brother. One look at his smirk and she took the challenge.

Logan grabbed her wrist to stop her. "Be honest with them, Mel. They're here to help you and to put a stop to the murders and the drug dealing."

She swallowed hard then whispered, "I trust you."

He smiled in return, and she climbed over Mick's long legs to get to the middle of the couch.

"Here's the deal. Our main intel tell us that there's a secret location and lab somewhere close to the city. The guy we had on the inside was getting close when he was killed. This location also acts as a kind of showroom for the types of drugs and distribution available and that Bret offers. We believe that there's another guy involved with this operation by the name of Miguel. He's been making his presence known on the streets and is said to have some major backers in Colombia and Mexico."

"What about that warehouse we raided last week? Did they get you any leads?" Sunny asked.

Melissa was trying to pay attention to what they were discussing when Mick moved closer.

She looked him in the eye, and he tried to give her some sexy stare down that was supposed to turn her on. She realized that it turned her off. There were only five wolves she was interested in, and right now they were watching her. Taking in Mick's good looks, she felt nothing. Beyond a little flirting here and there it seemed that the Valdamar men had ruined her.

"Good," she heard in her head, and she looked at the five of them. They stood with their arms crossed in front of their chests, and they didn't seem too fond of her sitting so close to these men.

"It was your idea," she stated through their link.

"Hey, Melissa, I've seen you dance before. I think it was at a bachelor party a couple of weeks back. You've got some great moves," Mick teased, looking over her cleavage and then sniffing her hair. She heard the low growls and knew her men were close-by if this wolf tried anything.

She sat back, re-crossed her legs, then stared at him.

"Hey, I think I do remember you," she whispered, and he smirked at his brothers who seemed to be annoyed at the game he was playing.

Mick leaned closer. "You do?" he asked then winked.

"Sure I do. I always remember the cheap tippers." The guys laughed, and Mick got up from the couch and cleared his throat.

"I was just messing with her," he replied.

"Yeah, well, fun and games are over. Let's get down to business," William replied.

"So this is the situation. We need to find the main manufacturing lab and this showroom. I've got people on Miguel, and Bret is hard to locate. He disappears the moment we're close to him. Being a wolf has its advantages."

"You can find Bret at the club. I'm working tomorrow night, and he usually plans a meeting with the other two guys you should be covering. Carlos Munos and Chico Ferone. There's also a third dealer. It's actually a family. They're from the Philippines."

"The Philippines?" Jake asked. She looked at him and nibbled her bottom lip.

"They are, but they have a Spanish last name. It's Fernandez."

William wrote down the names, and one of his other brothers left the room as he talked into his cell phone.

"Anything you can tell us about them? What's their involvement, and where do they get their drugs from?"

Melissa was hesitant a moment as the fear hit her gut. Vince moved next to her and touched her shoulder.

"Tell him, Mel, so we can move on with our lives and put all this bullshit behind you."

She found strength in his touch, and knowing that they loved her and wouldn't leave her gave her courage.

"I can tell you anything you want to know. But first I need to know that my children, my aunt, and my friend Celine will be protected."

"We've got guys covering them. They're safe and we will continue to protect them until this is over," William promised then smiled at her.

She immediately looked at Logan, and he nodded for her to trust William's word.

Taking a deep breath, Melissa began to explain about Bret's drug cartel and all the individuals involved with it. Then she gave the location of the secret laboratory and showroom they had mentioned, as well as names and locations of different suppliers. By the end of their conversation they were thanking Melissa and promising that they would establish a plan of attack.

* * * *

The Declan pack left the house, and Melissa crossed her arms in front of her chest and stared out the window. It was a done deal. She had officially snitched out the drug dealers and the bad guys. Her mates had watched her. They listened to her describe every detail and knowledge of Bret's operation that she knew. She had confessed to her methods of pulling off the hits. She had divulged the locations of the three most important aspects of Bret's operations as well as Carlos, Chico, and the Fernandez family. She couldn't stop shaking. She feared for her family although she was confident that Bret wouldn't find out that the information had come from her. Her other concern was Jamie. He had murdered her sister and brother-in-law, leaving three children without parents and sending them all into years of turmoil. Melissa had remained focused on the children and her aunt for all these years. She put so much pressure on herself to try and provide for her instant family. She was tired. It had taken Logan, Sunny, Jake, Frankie, and Vince entering her life for her to see all that she had missed and all that she would continue to give up. Could this really be the end of all the struggling with bills and security for her future and that of her family? Could these five men really love her and honestly be willing to take care of her and her family? The tears stung her eyes, and her heart ached with a mix of uncertainty and desperation for it to be true.

"It is true, and you belong to us now, Melissa. We love you," Logan stated through their link, and the others added their similar comments. She sobbed by the window, and then she felt big, strong arms go around her. Jake laid his head on her shoulder and kissed her cheek.

"Don't cry, baby. You're breaking my heart." He squeezed her, and she continued to cry.

"You've worked so hard, Mel. You've done so many great things, but the time has come to do what's right for you. We're in this together," he whispered then kissed the top of her head and held her firmly in his arms.

Melissa stared out the window at nothing in particular as she absorbed Jake's embrace.

"I've done some crazy stuff, Jake. I didn't realize just how much information I had picked up on over the last year. I hope that I haven't just written my own death sentence."

Jake immediately turned her around to face him. He touched his fingers to her chin, making her look up at him.

"You've done no such thing. It was the right thing to do for you, for us, and for your family."

"I'm scared," she confessed.

He caressed her cheek and smiled at her.

"Look at me, Melissa."

She did, and when she stared into his eyes, she saw him change from man to wolf, a protector of her body and soul. He sent his thoughts to her mind, and she understood the power he and his brothers possessed. She was in awe, but she held his gaze, and when he smiled, he revealed elongated incisors and a look that told her he could devour just about anything.

Melissa wasn't afraid. In fact she was turned on as she felt her body sway toward him as liquid drenched her panties. She reached up and gently touched his teeth. She was amazed at the way his face partially shifted from human man to Alpha wolf.

"We are all bonded to you just as you are bonded to us. Ask me anything you want to know and I will tell you," Jake stated. His voice sounded different because of the teeth.

"I'm wondering what it will feel like when your cock is deep inside my pussy, when you bring me to orgasm, as you all do so well, and you bite into me with teeth like that."

Jake growled as his lifted her up, she straddled his waist, and he pressed her against the wall.

It was fast, and he was in complete control as Jake ravished her mouth, sucking and pulling on her tongue. Melissa grabbed him and pulled at his shirt and tried to undo his pants as he had his way with her.

She loved the feel of those teeth against her neck. He was strong and powerful as he used his chest and one arm to hold her up while his other hand undid his pants. He was magnificent, and so darn sexy she lifted her skirt higher and ripped the thong she wore herself. She felt hungry for his cock and needy to be connected completely. With Jake inside her, she would feel complete. Whenever one of her mates was deep inside her, she felt most content. It was odd, and it was beautiful.

He growled against her ear as he pulled his cock from confinement and she helped him line it up with her pussy.

"Fuck!" he growled, pushing forward and shoving his dick deep into her cunt. It was crazy and wild and just the way she wanted it. Thrust for thrust his hips rocked forward and backward. In and out his cock hammered into her. She moaned and held on to his shoulders, biting his neck, his skin, and anything she could latch her mouth on. Melissa felt his cock grow bigger and thicker. Her vaginal muscles clung tight to the steely iron and caused her to gasp for air. Her body rocked orgasm after orgasm until Jake grabbed her ass, thrust down then up, penetrating her deeply before exploding inside her as he bit into her shoulder. Melissa growled her release and held on to Jake until he finished pumping into her.

She hadn't realized she was crying until Jake kissed her mouth.

"You taste salty," he murmured, and then he realized why.

He cupped her face between his manly hands and held her gaze.

"Did I hurt you?" he asked, and she half chuckled and half sobbed then placed her hands on his face just like he held her face.

"No. I just love you so damn much it's overwhelming."

Jake smiled then kissed her lips and held her tightly in his arms.

* * * *

Jake and Melissa were so wrapped up in the moment that they hadn't even known the others were there. Well, at least she hadn't noticed. When she looked over Jake's shoulder, the others were standing there watching them with smirks on their faces and desire in their eyes. But Frankie was twirling her ripped pair of black panties around his finger.

She blushed then pressed her face into Jake's neck as he turned around to see what had embarrassed her.

"Nice," he commented then pulled his cock from Melissa's body and slowly set her down.

"You okay?" he questioned with concern still, not taking his hands from her waist and being sure she was able to stand.

"You're not that good, Jake," Frankie teased.

Jake flipped Frankie off then picked his pants up off the floor.

Melissa grabbed a hold of Jake's shoulder and laid her head against his bicep as she looked directly at Frankie.

"Oh, yes, he is," she replied firmly, and Jake laughed, but Frankie looked at it as a challenge.

Frankie twirled her panties on one finger then used his other finger to point at her and curl it toward him, indicating for Melissa to come to him.

She felt her cheeks heat and her body warm up again as she slowly and seductively made her way to him.

* * * *

Frankie sat in the middle of the sectional with his legs wide open as he leaned back. Sunny sat on the end of the couch, Vince sat on the other end, and Logan stood behind Frankie. Seductively she crawled over Sunny, who issued her a nice smack to her ass before he undid the button on her skirt and pulled it from her body. She crawled out of it and straight to Frankie.

His eyes glowed, and she could tell she was turning him on.

* * * *

Frankie felt his cock push against the zipper of his pants, demanding release. But his little dancer was playing a game with him, and he wanted to see what she would do next. The way she allowed Jake to fuck her against the living room wall was hot. The way their emotions showed and how deep they felt the connection was a complete turn-on. He had to have her. His wolf needed to fuck her good, but all he could do right now was wait.

He held Melissa's gaze as she crawled over Sunny. Sunny removed her skirt, and Frankie could see her glistening cunt just waiting for his cock.

"I want my panties back," she whispered when she reached his thighs.

He swiftly pulled her toward him, wrapped his arms around her waist, and cupped both her ass cheeks.

"Is that all that you want from me?" he asked then pressed a finger over the crevice of her ass then to her sopping wet pussy.

She purred near his ear. "No. I want your big, hard cock, and I want it Frankie style."

That was it for Frankie.

He lifted her up so she straddled his waist, and he pulled her shirt up over her head, revealing her black lace bra.

"Get this off," he demanded as she raised her arms and began to unclip the back slowly in an attempt to torture him. At the same time he undid his pants, lifted her so she was on her knees, and pulled his pants off.

The sight of her swollen pussy lips drenched with her desire sent him over the edge. He lined his throbbing cock up to her entrance and pulled her down. Melissa removed her bra and tossed it, making it land on Vince.

Up and down, she rode him hard as Frankie bit her nipples and licked her breasts.

"Put your hands in the air and keep them there," he demanded, and immediately she raised her arms.

The sight of her beautiful body fucking him increased his need for more. The warmth of her cunt, the wetness coating his thighs, brought on his wolf. He felt his eyes change as he grabbed Melissa by her hips and thrust up into her.

Melissa moaned and closed her eyes. She looked like a goddess as her tits bounced in front of him and her ass hit his balls.

"Fuck yeah, Mel. Ride him good," Jake yelled.

She lifted her rear up and down, keeping her arms in the air, and Frankie lost it. He pulled her to him just as he thrust up into her and exploded inside of her.

They panted for air then he kissed her, bringing her hands behind her back and making her breasts press hard against his chest.

"I love you, mate."

"I love you, too," she whispered.

* * * *

Melissa sat up, and Frankie cupped her breasts. Then she felt herself being lifted up, and this time it was Logan.

He placed her body over the arm of the couch, lifted her hips, and pushed his cock inside her pussy from behind. There was no preamble, no words, no indication of anything other than the fact that he needed to fuck her.

Melissa felt his desire. She heard his thoughts and knew he couldn't even speak. He rocked his hips against her ass as he played with her ass cheeks, spreading them then squeezing them. Her body burned with need as she held herself up with her hands and took her loving from Logan.

Then she felt Vince kneeling next to her, and she saw his cock. The mushroom top glistened with pre-cum, and she licked her lips, prepared to suck him dry.

Logan grabbed a fistful of her hair and pushed forward in three deep, long strokes causing her to lose her breath.

Her lips parted, and Vince pushed forward. She sucked his cock into her mouth and tried to gain the same pace as Logan. But it was no use. The man was a muscle machine.

Instead, she allowed Logan and Vince to set the pace and have their way with her.

In and out, Vince fucked her mouth and caressed her hair.

"You're so sexy, Mel. I love everything about you."

He pushed deeper, and she took him inside, trying not to gag. Just when she felt like she could gag, he pulled back a little. He was a compassionate lover, so she sucked him harder. She wanted it to be good for him, and there were no more unhappy thoughts. She loved her men, and she loved their taste.

"I love her ass," Logan stated then slapped her cheeks, making her come again and again.

They increased their speed, and Vince came first, shooting his essence down her throat as she swallowed every ounce of him.

Vince pulled from her mouth then kissed her lips as he caressed her back and then her ass cheeks.

Logan lifted her up around the waist and thrust his hips harder and faster. In this position he got deeper penetration as Melissa held on for the ride.

Then Sunny kneeled in front of her and played with her breasts, cupping them and fondling them as Logan thrust harder, nearly sending her into Sunny.

She heard Logan growl against her neck, then she felt him explode inside of her as the aftershocks rocked their bodies.

Sunny got up off the couch as Logan pulled from her pussy. Immediately he locked his arm around her waist as he kissed her shoulder blades then her spine.

"I love you, mate," he whispered.

"I love you, too," she replied.

Then she felt Sunny gently press her chest to the couch and spread her thighs. She wasn't certain what he would do next, but she was sensationally sore and quite tired from their lovemaking. Then she felt his warm, wet tongue touch her pussy lips and she moaned. Her body revved up all over again as Sunny pressed a finger into her pussy then pulled it back out. He licked her labia and swirled his tongue around her pussy lips, making her cream herself more.

Then she felt his finger leave her, and she anticipated his next move.

Slowly he lined his cock with her pussy from behind and pressed forward as he held his palms against her back and waist.

With every slow, deep, penetrating thrust, she felt her muscles grab his cock. She wanted more. She craved it harder, so she lifted her ass and thrust back against him.

Sunny chuckled. Although she couldn't see his face from her position, she imagined his stern expression and his shoulder-length hair. Her untamable wolf and his enormous cock.

His fingers played with her ass cheeks, spreading them wider then pressing a finger against the hole.

She thrust back against him, and he gave her ass a smack then thrust against her harder.

Sunny pulled back on her hips and ran his hands under her arms to her breasts. He rocked against her then pulled her nipples before massaging her breasts some more.

"My beautiful dancer. Your body is a work of art," he whispered then increased his speed.

Melissa moaned against him then asked for more.

"Harder, Sunny, please, I need." She panted, and he thrust into her faster, taking her body to the next level. She felt his fingers play with her puckered hole, and then he thrust faster and faster, harder and harder into her from behind. Her body rocked and tightened up. She was almost there when suddenly he pressed his finger into her puckered hole, and she screamed her release into the couch. Sunny thrust a few more hard, fast times then exploded inside of her.

He lay his face against her back and kissed her shoulder and then her spine.

"Incredible," he whispered before pulling from her.

It was Logan who lifted her up into his arms and carried her upstairs to the bathroom shower.

Chapter 17

"The raid is taking place tomorrow night. Melissa said that's when Bret and the other drug dealers she mentioned host a party to showcase their drugs and the high quality. It will be a simultaneous raid. We're going to hit all four locations at exactly the same time and wipe out the entire operation," Willy told Logan over the cell phone. Logan had it on speaker so that he, Frankie, Sunny, and Jake could hear the information.

Melissa was in the bathroom drying her hair and talking to Vince.

"We understand, and we'll be set to go in there, too," Frankie added.

"What about Melissa and her family? I've got a team in there now protecting the apartment. They haven't seen a sign of anything," Willy stated.

"She's going into work tonight. It's her last shift, and she promised not to be late and to call if Bret shows up. Although I'm hoping he'll be right in the middle of that showroom when we gas his ass and shoot the place to shit," Sunny added.

"That will be great. I'm sure she'll be fine because he has no idea what is going on. But she should be extra careful. She's a beautiful woman, and I wouldn't want her out of my sight if she were my mate," Willy added.

"Those are our feelings exactly. But she has to give notice, and she has to show up for work tonight. Her bartender friend Tara is going onstage for the first time. Then she's done," Frankie stated firmly.

"Okay. I'll call you back with all the details. Maybe while Melissa is at work we can go over the blueprints of the place and figure out which teams will hit which first. I've got people watching the place now."

"That sounds good, Willy. Call us after nine o'clock," Logan replied then hung up the phone.

Melissa came out of the bathroom holding Vince's hand and wearing her uniform for Charlie's club. The tight skirt, the high heels, and the sexy top had all their wolves in turmoil. They glared at her without realizing it as they absorbed the way her shirt lifted, revealing her belly ring. Not happening.

She placed her hands on her hips and raised her eyebrows in challenge.

"Now, come on, it's only one more night."

Jake walked over to her and placed his arms around her waist from behind. He kissed her neck and sniffed her hair, making her giggle. His arms pushed against her breasts, but then his hands grabbed her shirt and pulled it lower and over her belly ring.

Jake turned her towards him and looked at her.

"A little better, but still too sexy for anyone's eyes but ours."

She chuckled then began to walk toward the doorway.

"Not so fast. We have a few things to go over with you," Sunny told her as he took her hand and brought her over to the bed. He sat down then pulled her onto his right leg. She sat there sideways as she placed her arm over his shoulder and listened to their rules.

Glancing at her watch, she became impatient.

"Okay, I got it. I promise to call you every hour if I'm not crazy busy. I promise to call you if Bret shows up or if I get scared, nervous, or unsure of somebody in the club."

Sunny kissed her again then released her to his brothers. One by one they kissed her before they walked her out to her car.

* * * *

"I can't believe that you're going to be leaving us," Tara complained with tears in her eyes. She hugged Melissa, and Melissa felt herself getting emotional as well. That was exactly everyone's response when she arrived at work tonight. They were happy to see her move on, but they were sad to lose a good friend.

"You're on in twenty minutes, sweetheart," Charlie told Tara as he squeezed Tara's shoulders and smiled.

Tara looked a bit nervous, but she was ready.

"You'll do great, Tara," Melissa encouraged her friend as she watched Tara walk out from behind the bar then toward the dressing room.

"The place is really hopping tonight. Melissa yelled over the loud music.

"It sure is. I think Tara already has a following."

"That's great!" Melissa exclaimed as she washed some of the beer mugs then placed them on the drying rack.

A few guys came to the bar, and she got their orders, flirted with them a bit, and served their beers.

"You're a real charmer, Mel. I'm going to miss you," Charlie complained as she returned to stand beside him.

He had tears in his eyes, and she was shocked.

"Don't you get all emotional on me. It's not like I'm leaving town."

"Yeah, like you'll stop in to see us some time? Those men of yours won't let you out of their sight or near this place."

She chuckled.

"You're right. They won't. As a matter of fact I need to text them. I'm supposed to check in with them."

"There you go. I'm surprised they even allowed you to come back here."

"And what, sweep me off to another country along with my kids and my aunt? That's not happening, Charlie. That only happens in those fiction romance novels."

Charlie laughed.

"So are were wolves and vampires?" he teased, and she laughed then got serious.

"Vampires are real, too?"

Charlie laughed so hard he began to cough, and Melissa wasn't sure she got a response.

She would have to ask the guys about that one.

Her cell phone beeped, and she reached down to check the message.

You're ten minutes late. Is everything okay? Logan

Yes. I was talking with Tara. She's going on next. I may be late texting you because the place is busy. By the way, do vampires exist, too?

If you meet any vampires stay the fuck away from them. Unless his name is Carlyle. Logan.

Melissa laughed then wondered if he was kidding.

Melissa served some more beers as Johnny, the other bartender joined her. They talked about the night and how crowded it was for a weekday, and then they heard the drumroll and Charlie's voice.

Just then he announced that Tara was making her debut appearance. The crowd roared and the music began as Tara took the stage.

Melissa watched her strut her stuff, and she was very impressed. The guys loved her whole roaring twenties routine.

Melissa leaned against the door to the backroom as everyone's attention focused on the stage. That's when she saw Jamie enter the club and make his way around the bar. He spotted her immediately, and she panicked.

She reached for her cell phone and began to text Logan.

Jamie is here. I'm getting Spike.

She signaled to Spike, but he was caught in the crowd watching Tara.

"Mel! I want to talk to you."

"I have nothing to say to you, Jamie."

"Well, I've got something to say to you."

He walked under the opening at the end of the bar and grabbed her. He took her by her wrist and dragged her out of the room. No one seemed to notice. She was about to scream when she felt the barrel of his gun against her rib cage.

"Why are you doing this?" she asked in fear as he quickly walked her to the back room.

The room was dark as he pressed her body against the wall.

"Stop it, Jamie. I'm not interested." She pushed against him, and he pressed the gun hard against her ribs.

Her phone immediately began to ring, and Jamie switched on the light switch. Her eyes adjusted to the light, and her mouth dropped open at the sight of Bret and Chu standing there waiting.

She reached for the phone, but Jamie pulled it from her waist and looked at the number.

"Valdamar!" he exclaimed then placed it on the ground and crushed the phone.

"I know you've met my acquaintances," Jamie stated, pressing her harder against the wall and holding her there by her throat.

Melissa felt the tears reach her eyes. They were going to kill her.

"What do you want from me?" She barely got the words out.

"My friends have some questions for you," Jamie stated as Chu approached.

She looked toward Bret and his smug expression then toward Chu.

"They want to know why you've been hanging around the Valdamar pack, and why William Declan paid you a visit about some extra money you came into, Mel," Jamie stated.

"I don't know what you're talking about," Melissa replied, and Jamie squeezed her throat tighter. Instinctively she raised her hands and gripped his wrists. She felt her windpipe tighten. He would choke her to death.

"Where did you get the money?" he demanded to know then loosened his grip on her neck.

"Stripping," she whispered, and Bret's eyes widened.

"I've never seen you strip, Mel." Bret chimed in as he approached them. He eyed her from toes to head then licked his lips.

"That's a lot of money to get from stripping," Chu added, and she gave him a dirty look. He was scum, too.

"Not for Lola Lamore," she blurted out.

Again the men were shocked. They looked her body over as if they would know what she would look like as a blonde wearing hardly anything.

"It doesn't matter. We don't have time for this. Obviously, the money isn't yours, Bret. So if you don't mind, my woman and I will be going. We have a plane to catch."

"What?" Melissa exclaimed as she tried to pull away from Jamie.

In an instant, Chu reached for the gun, and the two men struggled for its possession.

Melissa tried to run, but Bret grabbed her by her hair and pulled her back against his chest.

She reached up to hold his hand to get him to release her when she heard a growl and then a gun going off.

She screamed, and when Bret turned her around, Jamie was standing there holding the gun, and a few feet away was a very large animal. It looked like a big, ugly dog, and then it showed its fangs, and she attempted to pull away.

The animal growled, and Jamie screamed then fired the gun again. In an instant, the beast attacked Jamie, ripping out his throat as blood scattered across the room.

Melissa attempted to run, but Bret dragged her by her hair and headed toward the doorway.

She kicked and screamed, trying to fight against Bret when she heard him growl and saw his eyes change.

"Don't piss me off, Mel. You're coming with me."

He kicked the back door open, setting off the alarms as he pulled her across the parking lot.

Bret shoved her against the limo and her chin hit the doorframe.

She cried out in pain, and when she turned to fight Bret off again, he struck her in the head with something.

Suddenly, she felt pain and then darkness.

* * * *

"The raid is in motion now. Our inside people say it's going down tonight," Willy told Logan over the phone.

"Okay, we're on our way. We'll have to get someone over to Mel. I don't want her in that club when the shit hits the fan," Logan stated just as his phone buzzed.

"Wait. I've got a text from Mel."

"Oh, fuck. We got to move. Mel says that Jamie is at the club."

"What?" Frankie asked as he pulled on his gear.

"We have to get to Mel, Willy," Logan stated.

"Go! I'll call in team four. Keep me updated."

Logan hung up the phone and grabbed the keys to the truck.

"If that fucker hurts her, he's a dead man," Sunny exclaimed as they all ran out to the truck.

* * * *

Ten minutes later, they arrived on the scene at Charlie's. There were police cars everywhere and a special operations unit in the back parking lot. All the patrons were exiting the club and getting into their vehicles.

The men showed their badges and rushed inside, trying to find Melissa.

They called to her through their link and got no response.

They saw Charlie just as he saw them.

"He got her, guys. I can't fucking believe this, but he got her."

"Who got her, Jamie?" Vince asked.

"No. Bret."

"Oh, fuck!" Sunny exclaimed.

"What the fuck happened?" Jake demanded to know, and Charlie explained.

They checked out the crime scene and showed their IDs to the men who secured the backroom. They were wolves, and they had to ensure that no humans saw what had occurred in the back room. Luckily, Charlie had heard the gunfire and ran in there first. He knew enough to secure the room and evacuate the building.

They talked to the men in charge as they absorbed the scene. Jamie lay dead on the floor, covered in blood with his throat ripped out. They knew that a wolf was the culprit. A few feet away, another man lay in half shift. It was Chu, Bret's right-hand man and bodyguard. He had multiple bullet wounds to his chest and shoulder. Obviously too many to shift and save him. He was dead, too.

"This is a big fucking mess, Logan," one of the investigators complained.

"You're telling me, but it gets worse. The man who this guy works for has our mate. Any indication of which way they headed?" Logan asked.

"Your fucking mate? Shit, Logan, what do you need? I've got guys everywhere on standby for some secret multi-raid thing going on in New Jersey and here."

"Yeah, it's all part of the same situation. We're going to head out. We need to find where Bret took her."

Logan walked through the mess and into the back parking lot. He looked around the ground and sniffed the air. His brothers were right there with him.

"I smell her blood," Frankie stated in a growl.

"Right here," Sunny added as he bent down and touched his finger to the blacktop.

He brought it to his nose.

"Is it Mel's?" Vince asked.

He nodded.

"Fuck!" Frankie replied.

"Where could he have taken her?" Jake asked out loud.

"I don't know but the first place we have to look is his home. Let's go," Logan commanded, and they ran toward their truck.

They headed out of Manhattan and across the George Washington Bridge to New Jersey. They knew that the location of Bret's house was somewhere near where the showroom was.

"I hope to the gods we find her before he hurts her," Frankie said. The others added similar comments.

"I tried to contact her through our link and got no response," Vince told his brothers.

"We all did, and nothing," Sunny said then banged his fist on the dashboard.

"We should have never let her go, man. We should have made her stay with us," Frankie spoke as he ran his fingers through his hair. The helpless feeling filled them all.

* * * *

"Team three, I have a visual on another vehicle entering the maid's quarters on the right side of the estate. Please confirm our guest and add them to the list," Mick stated through his headset as he watched the house and building through his binoculars, waiting for the order to go in. So far, six high-profile drug dealers entered the showroom and party. None had left.

"That's a negative on the vehicle, sir. I have a large tree in my way and a male and female guest fucking against it. Maybe you can assist?"

They laughed over the airway, and Mick crawled backward to get into a better position as he spoke softly into the mouthpiece.

"I got it covered. Just try not to lose your focus. The call will come in any minute."

Just then, Mick had the limo and its occupants in view. His heart hammered in his chest. There was Bret lifting a voluptuous brunette with a perfectly round ass out of the limo. When he tossed her over his shoulder, Mick immediately recognized her.

"Fuck, commander! I got a fucking visual, and it ain't good!"

"What do you got, Mick?" Willy asked, sounding concerned.

"I got team two's woman. It's Mel, and she's unconscious and bleeding from her head."

"Son of a bitch. I'm on it. Keep her in your sights."

"They entered the house, Commander. What's your order?"

"We move in seven minutes. Fernandez family en route and in the vicinity."

"Out."

* * * *

Willy banged his fist on the dashboard inside the SWAT team surveillance truck. They had the place surrounded and all other locations in position on his command to enter.

He called Logan.

* * * *

"Hey, Willy, what do you got?" Logan answered his phone, hoping that Willy had a lead on Bret. "I got a visual on your mate."

"What?" Frankie yelled.

William explained the situation and told the men where their position would be and to get there in six minutes. Logan stepped on the gas and ditched the car two blocks from the location. They grabbed their gear, put on their headsets, and ran to meet Mick and the rest of the team.

As soon as they arrived, they got into position and watched the house.

They waited for Willy's order.

* * * *

Melissa rolled her head back and forth. The pain was excruciating. She blinked her eyes and tried to focus on where she was. When she tried to lift her hand to her face to rub her eyes, she couldn't move them. She was tied to a bed. Looking down, she saw that she was only wearing a bra and panties and her legs were loose.

"Ahh, Sleeping Beauty finally awakes. Or should I say Miss Robin Hood." Bret chuckled as he rose from the chair. He held a snifter of brandy in his hand, and all he was wearing was a silk robe. She prayed that he was fully dressed under there.

"Let me loose, Bret. You've lost your mind."

He placed the glass down on the bedside table then stared at her body.

"I missed you, Mel. Fucking you once and never having you again was like torture."

He ran a finger over her thigh then to her mound. She kicked her legs at him, forcing his hand away.

"There's no need to fight it. You're mine now, and tomorrow we head out to the coast. Oh, and don't worry about the little brats and the old lady. They'll be dead in about ten minutes," he stated smugly as he glanced at his wristwatch.

"You fucking bastard. Don't you touch them! I'll never be yours!" she screamed then cried in fear for her children and aunt. She prayed that Willy and his men protected them as they promised.

"Now is that any way to talk to your Alpha?" he teased then leaned down to lick her lips. She spit at him, and he backhanded her across the mouth.

She tasted the blood, and she felt the pain in her jaw as she tried to pull on her restraints.

"Don't touch me!" she screamed, losing her voice as the rope cut her skin on her wrist.

In a flash, Bret was on top of her. He straddled her hips, and she cried out for help.

"We're here. Just hold steady."

She heard Logan's voice and gasped. They were here, and they would save her, just like they promised. Her heart pounded in her chest as Bret leaned forward and licked her cleavage.

"Get off of me, you idiot. I'll never be yours," she yelled, and he hit her again. She thought she saw stars. It was such a hard hit. It took her a moment to refocus. Anger filled her body as the tears rolled down her cheeks.

"You're going to be my mate, my woman, forever."

"Never! I will never be yours because I belong to the Valdamar pack. My men are my mates, and they will find you and kill you!" She clenched her teeth and spit at him again.

His eyes changed color, and his incisors elongated before her. She felt the claws by her ribs. Then he grabbed her arms and cut her skin.

Melissa screamed just as the sound of glass shattering filled the room. Out of nowhere, she saw multiple things fly into Bret. Then she heard growling and fighting as she tried to get free. Melissa was so scared she cried and screamed until she heard the howl and then a torturous sound fill the room.

She closed her eyes and continued to cry in pain and fear until she felt the hand against her stomach. She jerked her body. "You're safe, Melissa. Your men are here." She opened her eyes and saw Mick. Her chest heaved up and down. Then she felt the fingers at her wrists undoing the ropes. Looking up, she saw Frankie and Vince. They caressed her hands and gently brought her arms down cursing at the damage to her forearms and to her face and head.

She closed her eyes and cried until she felt all her men around her, touching her.

"I'll get a first aid kit. Don't move her yet," Mick whispered then rose from the bed.

* * * *

Logan and Sunny shifted back to human form and fixed their clothing. They tried to calm their breathing, but they were still fired up and on the defensive. Logan had freaked out hearing what Bret was doing to Mel while they waited for the order. When she cried out in pain, they had to move in. All he saw was red as the anger filled his wolf and the need to protect his mate took precedence over everything else. Logan ripped Bret's throat out as his brother Sunny cut his claws across Bret's chest.

"You're going to be okay, Mel. We got you now," Vince whispered as he placed his hand over her belly. It seemed to be the one place besides her legs that wasn't cut or bruised.

Frankie did the same, and then Jake kissed her lips, being sure to not get too close to the cut there.

"Is she okay?" Logan asked.

"I'm okay because of all of you," Mel replied as the tears rolled down her cheeks.

Sunny touched her ankle just as Mick returned with the first aid kit. In the distance, they heard the gunfire and the sound of sirens fill the air. The simultaneous raids were going on all over the place from New Jersey to Manhattan.

The men tended to her wounds. Mick got her something to wear. Then they carried her out of the house to take her home.

"What about the kids? Are they okay? He said he had someone there to kill them," Melissa asked, filled with concern.

"They're fine. We had team four nearby and they intervened. They'll be waiting at the hospital," Jake added.

"I'm not going to the hospital," she refused.

"The hell you're not. You have a cut that needs stitches and possibly a concussion. Never mind the scratches to your forearms and that nasty cut lip. You will go and that is final," Frankie ordered, and she huffed and puffed, causing pain to radiate through her body. She closed her eyes and let her men take care of her.

Epilogue

Melissa stood by the picture window looking out toward the grassy area near the woods. Her mates were teaching Brandon and Lea some strategic defense moves while Aunt Peggy sat in a garden chair watching Tommy throw a basketball into the hoop.

Everything had worked out just fine. They were a family, and her mates would teach the children about their heritage and about all the necessary training they needed.

She tapped the envelope against her lip, and its contents didn't seem as important anymore. She had everything she could ever want. Logan, Vince, Frankie, Jake, and Sunny were five wonderful, handsome, strong men who loved her. She had three children to raise and another on the way. She smiled to herself. The men were going to flip out. So this letter telling her if she passed the bar exam or not didn't mean as much as she first had thought it would. She wanted to start a family. She wanted the best for her children. Her Aunt Peggy, the sneaky woman, knew all along that the children were wolves, that her niece married a wolf, and that the Valdamar were wolves and Melissa's mates. So all those nights worrying about how to explain the relationship was wasted stress. But it gave her the strength and determination to achieve her degree and take the exam.

She looked at the envelope and imagined her men, and when she closed her eyes, she saw their handsome faces and she touched her belly. A baby was growing inside of her.

"Whoohoo!"

Melissa jumped at the sound of men yelling and hollering then stomping through the kitchen door and straight into the living room.

As soon as she locked gazes with them, she realized they had heard her thoughts.

Placing her hands on her hips, she gave them the evil eye, but they didn't hesitate to approach as Sunny lifted her into his arms and squeezed her tight. He kissed her then passed her to Frankie, who kissed her, too. They continued to pass her around. Vince held her tight as Jake caressed her hair and kissed her neck.

It was Logan who stood there with a serious expression on his face.

"Stop twirling her around like that. You might hurt the baby."

Jake laughed, and so did Vince.

"This is great, Mel. When did you find out?" Sunny asked, smiling. By now, the kids and her aunt had joined the celebration. They were thrilled.

"I've known since yesterday."

"Yesterday?" Jake exclaimed.

Logan cleared his throat and stared at her. She knew that look, and she knew just what to do. Slowly, she walked toward him, wrapped her arms around his neck, and kissed him.

He kissed her in return then released her so he could look into her eyes.

His large hand touched her belly. Then Frankie touched her belly as well as Jake, Vince, and Sunny from behind her. When she reached to cover their hands with her own, she realized she still held the envelope in her hands.

"What's that?" Vince asked.

"My results from the bar exam."

"Well?" Aunt Peggy chimed in, smiling and eliciting some chuckles from the guys.

She was silent a moment before she spoke.

"Mel?" Sunny whispered against her neck. The feel of her mates touching her and being so close as well as her aunt and the children brought joy to her heart.

"It doesn't matter. I have everything I want right here." She smiled and felt her mates' love through their link.

"That may be so, young lady, but I still want to know," Aunt Peggy exclaimed impatiently, and they all laughed.

"I passed!" Melissa replied, and everyone cheered.

"Looks like we have a lot to celebrate. I'm going to cook up a feast," Jake exclaimed then kissed her cheek.

"I'm helping you, Uncle Jake," Brandon exclaimed.

"Me, too," Lea added.

"Then let's get moving."

They all hurried into the kitchen, and when Melissa went to help, Sunny stopped her and pulled her into his arms.

"You are going to sit right here and rest. You've been studying like crazy for that test, and you have a baby to take care of."

She laughed as he lifted her feet and placed them on the stool.

Jake smiled at her as he and Lea began chopping up vegetables while Brandon climbed the chair and pulled spices from the closet.

Her aunt tended to Tommy, grabbing him a plate of crackers before she cut some cheese to go along with the crackers.

Vince placed a glass of water on the table for her then took out a couple of beers for his brothers.

Frankie began to set the table, and Logan put his arms around her as he teased Jake about some game they played with the kids outside.

It was all so wonderful. Melissa never thought life could be perfect. She wasn't even sure what the future might bring, but today she had her family, she had her life mates and their baby growing inside of her, and she loved them with all her heart.

THE END

WWW.DIXIELYNNDWYER.COM

ABOUT THE AUTHOR

People seem to be more interested in my name than where I get my ideas for my stories from. So I might as well share the story behind my name with all my readers.

My Momma was born and raised in New Orleans. At the age of twenty she met and fell in love with an Irishman named Patrick Riley Dwyer. Needless to say, the family was a bit taken aback by this as they hoped she would marry a family friend. It was a modern day arranged marriage kind of thing and my Momma downright refused.

Being that my Momma's families were descendents of the original English speaking southerners, they wanted the family blood line to stay pure. They were wealthy and my father's family was poor.

Despite attempts by my grandpapa to make Patrick leave and destroy the love between them, my parents married. They recently celebrated their sixtieth wedding anniversary.

I am one of six children born to Patrick and Lynn Dwyer. I am a combination of both Irish and a true southern belle. With a name like Dixie Lynn Dwyer it's no wonder why people are curious about my name.

Just as my parents had a love story of their own I grew up intrigued by the lifestyles of others. My imagination as well as my need to stray from the straight and narrow made me into the woman I am today.

Enjoy my newest series FIVE-O.

~Dixie~

Also by Dixie Lynn Dwyer

Siren Publishing, Inc.
www.SirenPublishing.com

CPSIA information can be obtained
at www.ICGtesting.com
Printed in the USA
LVOW04s0037060216

473972LV00023B/387/P